PRAISE FOR A

'I enjoyed every second and barely put it down! Another great horsey read from one of my favourite pony authors.'

'I wish all teen books were more like Flick Henderson and the Deadly Game. It is a terrific read, with a twisty, engaging plot, just enough romance and lots of pets. I'm only sad I've finished reading it - bring back Flick!'

'Absolutely love this author.'

TROPHY HORSE

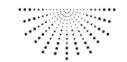

AMANDA WILLS

DISAPPEARING ACT

*K*risty Moore stared at the outfit hanging on her wardrobe door, her heart fluttering in her chest like a hyperactive butterfly. Pearly-white jodhpurs, courtesy of her friend Sofia, who had outgrown them the previous summer. Midnight blue fitted jacket, courtesy of her mum, who'd found it at the back of her own wardrobe, a relic from the days when she had attended glamorous cocktail parties with Kristy's dad.

'You might as well use it as a riding jacket,' her mum had said, fingering the silky material with a faraway look in her eyes. Since her dad had lost his job and they'd been forced to sell their four bedroomed house and move to a cramped apartment on the other side of town, their tiny mantelpiece had been bereft of a single gold-edged party invitation.

Under the jacket was Kristy's white school shirt. The final touch was a red, gold, blue and black striped tie. This was Norah's work. She'd spotted the ties in their local department store and bought four, one for each of the quadrille team.

'They're our colours,' she'd said, as she'd produced them

with a flourish while they'd been sipping their usual hot chocolates in the tack room after evening stables the previous week.

'Our *colours?*' said her twin brother William, his face screwed up.

'Red for Sofia to match her hair and gold for me, to match mine,' said Norah patiently. 'Blue for you because you're a boy and black for Cassius, of course.'

Kristy bit her lip but said nothing. It was as if she didn't exist. She knew Norah hadn't wanted her in the team from the outset, but she thought she had finally been accepted. Apparently not.

Kristy picked up a jodhpur boot and gave it a final buff with her sleeve. Her mum poked her head around the door.

'Shouldn't you have left by now? It's nearly twenty past ten.'

Kristy dropped the boot on her toe and yelped. The film crew was coming at eleven. That gave her precisely sixty seconds to get changed if she stood any chance of being at the stables in time to groom Cassius and be tacked up and ready for filming.

Kristy's mum must have registered the look of panic that swept across her face.

'I'll ask Dad if he can run you over, shall I?'

Kristy shot her a grateful smile and wriggled out of her jeans. 'Thanks Mum.'

Sofia's white jodhpurs fitted like a second skin and the tailored cocktail jacket, with its velvet collar and fitted waist, could easily have passed for a proper show jacket. Kristy fixed her tie, pulled on her riding gloves and inspected herself in the mirror.

'Not too shabby at all,' she said with satisfaction. She flicked her hair, narrowed her eyes and pursed her lips, a perfect impression of a disgruntled Norah. 'Apart from the tie,' she told her reflection in Norah's bossy tones. 'I think it's gaudy. The colours *clash*.'

She poked her tongue out at her reflection, the butterflies forgotten. If it hadn't been for Kristy they wouldn't have had a quadrille team, let alone won the competition at the Mayor's New Year's Eve show. No, if Norah was thinking she could revert to type and start lording it over Kristy she could think again.

~

'OK IF I DROP YOU HERE?' said Kristy's dad as he indicated right and pulled into the driveway of Mill Farm Stables.

''Course it is.' Kristy gathered her hat and gloves from the footwell.

'You alright? You look a bit pasty.'

'Bit nervous,' said Kristy. 'I don't want to let Cassius down.'

Her dad patted her knee. 'You'll be fine. Just pretend the cameras aren't there and be yourself. Have they told you when you'll be on?'

'Tonight, I think.'

'I'd better tape it. Gran'll want to see your five minutes of fame.'

Kristy rolled her eyes. 'People don't tape stuff any more, Dad. They *record* it. Onto their hard drive.'

He chuckled. 'Whatever. Oh, I almost forgot. I've got something for Cassius.' He reached into the glove compartment and pulled out a large carrot. 'Ta da!'

'Thanks.' Kristy checked her watch. It was gone half past ten. 'Gotta go! Tell Mum I'll be back for tea.'

Kristy held the carrot in one hand and her gloves and riding hat in the other and set off towards Mill Farm Stables. The contours of the long gravel driveway were as familiar to

3

her as her own face and she sidestepped puddles and ridges of loose chippings on autopilot, her thoughts on the ordeal ahead.

It had been Norah's idea. And, like most of Norah's ideas, by the time she happened to mention it to the rest of them it was a done deal.

'I've invited the BBC to send a film crew over to do a piece on the team,' she'd told them the previous week.

'You've done *what?*' exploded William.

'And they're coming next week,' she continued.

'Cool,' said Sofia.

'Did you not think to ask us first?' said Kristy.

'I think you'll find that as team leader I am well within my rights to organise a teeny bit of publicity.'

'We don't need publicity,' said William.

Norah ignored him. 'So I've said we'll perform a section of the routine and they'll probably want to interview me afterwards. It's only for the local news. I don't know what the problem is,' she huffed.

'You know my mates already take the mickey because I ride. I'll be crucified if we're on the telly,' William glowered.

'Do you want me to sort them out?' said Norah.

'And that is going to help how, exactly?' But William's mouth was twitching and Kristy could see Norah had won him round.

Sofia nudged Kristy in the ribs. 'Come on, it'll be fun.'

Kristy sighed. 'I suppose.'

And, through the sheer force of her personality, Norah got her way. Again.

The throaty growl of a powerful engine cut into Kristy's musings and she looked up to see a red convertible bearing down on her.

'Hey! Slow down!' she cried, waving her hands in front of her. But the car showed no sign of braking as it lurched over

the pitted driveway like a supercharged rally car. Kristy leapt into a hawthorn hedge as the car raced past, splattering muddy water over her pearly-white jodhpurs and snapping the carrot in two.

She stared at the broken carrot in disbelief.

'Idiot!' she cried, waggling it furiously. But the man in the sports car, crouched low over the steering wheel, his face hidden by a baseball cap and mirrored shades, offered no apologetic wave or dip of the head. She might as well have been invisible.

∼

KRISTY'S HEART sank when she saw Norah was already tacking up Silver. The other girl did a double take when she saw Kristy's mud-splattered jodhpurs.

'You're kidding me, right? You can't seriously be planning to wear *those*?'

Kristy took a deep breath and unclenched her jaw.

'I don't actually have much choice, seeing as they're the only pair I have with me. It's not my fault some twit in a red sports car was driving like a maniac and covered me in mud.'

Sofia poked her head over Jazz's stable door. 'Oh dear,' she giggled. 'Shall I see if Emma's got a spare pair?'

'You're a star,' said Kristy gratefully.

'They're due in twenty minutes and you haven't even caught Cassius yet,' Norah grumbled.

Kristy held up her hands. 'I know. I'll be quick, I promise.'

She grabbed Cassius's headcollar and lead rope from the tack room and sprinted down to the bottom paddock, the mangled carrot in her hand. Reaching the gate, she whistled impatient to throw her arms around Cassius and breathe in his familiar, horsey smell.

Usually he wandered over to the gate the minute she whistled, but today he was nowhere to be seen.

'Cassius!' she called softly, her eyes scanning his paddock. Sometimes he liked to doze in the bottom corner, but he wasn't there today. He wasn't behind the big oak tree either.

'Weird,' said Kristy, wondering if Emma had already brought him in and she'd walked straight past him. But he would have heard her and whickered, he always did.

A prickle of fear, like the sting of a wasp, sent goose-bumps down her spine. Where was he?

'Cassius!' she called again, her voice rising an octave. Still there was no sign of the big, black Percheron. Kristy scanned the field one last time and ran back up to the stables, almost colliding with Sofia, who was holding up a pair of cream jodhpurs.

'These'll have to do, they're all Emma had.'

'Did one of you bring Cassius in?' said Kristy breathlessly.

Sofia shook her head. 'Why, what's the matter?'

'He's not in the field.' Kristy threw open his stable door but it was empty. 'And he's not in his stable.' She gripped Sofia's arm until the older girl winced. 'Where *is* he?'

2
CELEBRITY STATUS

ofia eased Kristy's fingers open one by one. 'I'm sure he can't have gone far. Why don't I check the barn and you go and ask Emma. Maybe she's put him in a different paddock.'

'There are no other paddocks!' wailed Kristy.

She knocked on Emma's back door and let herself into the boot room. 'Emma?' she called, picking her way over the heap of wellies positioned like a booby trap just inside. A tub of minerals balanced precariously on the long shelf above the chipped stone sink and half a dozen creakily-stiff Barbour jackets in various shades of brown and green hung from a row of hooks in front of her. Bert, Emma's cantankerous Persian cat, eyed her grumpily from his bed above the boiler.

Kristy loved Emma's boot room. Her mum would be aghast at the tangle of cobwebs that festooned the ceiling like spidery paper chains, and the layers of dirt and horse hair that had turned the once-white floor tiles the colour of parchment. Kristy's mum was so house proud she polished and dusted every other day and plumped up the sofa cushions the minute you stood up. Emma said housework was for people who didn't have horses. Her house was messy, homely and always smelt ever-so-slightly of wet horse.

The horse smell was stronger than ever today, Kristy thought, as she stretched a hand up to stroke Bert and then thought better of it when his tail swished crossly.

'Emma!' she called again, kicking off her boots and pushing open the door to the kitchen. Her hand flew to her mouth.

'Oh!'

Cassius was standing between Emma's scrubbed pine table and the sink, his black ears pricked. Kristy closed her eyes and shook her head. Surely she must be dreaming? He whickered and her eyes snapped open. No, it really was him. Giddy with relief, she could only grip the table and mumble, 'There you are!'

Cassius squeezed his huge frame through the gap towards her and snaffled the carrot from her hand.

'You rascal,' Kristy said fondly, scratching his poll. 'We'd better get you out of here before Emma sees you.'

The black gelding followed her out of the kitchen, through the boot room and across a small patch of lawn to the yard. A dusty white estate car was reversing next to Emma's Land Rover.

'KRISTEEEE!' shrieked Norah. 'They're here! You've got literally five minutes to get ready!'

'You found him then,' said Sofia, handing Kristy Emma's old jodhpurs.

'You'll never guess where.'

'No time for chat!' Norah screeched.

'She's a nightmare,' said William, dumping Cassius's grooming kit at their feet and running his fingers through his unruly blond hair. 'I'll give you a hand.'

Kristy darted into the tack room to change. Something

was bugging her but she didn't have time to think about it now. Norah was already on the warpath. She'd go mad if Kristy wasn't ready in time. Emma's old jodhpurs smelt of mothballs and were at least three sizes too big. Kristy glanced longingly at the mud-splattered pair she'd shed like a snake skin on the floor and then looked down at Emma's cast-offs, which flared at her hips and wrinkled around her ankles like a melted candle. If this was an omen, she thought glumly, it did not bode well.

~

A FRECKLY GIRL WITH LONG, auburn hair was lugging a camera out of the boot of the car. She lifted it onto her shoulder with practised ease.

'Ruth,' she said, holding out her free hand. 'Pleased to meet you.'

'But where are the others?' said Norah, her hands on her hips.

'This is it, I'm afraid. We self-shoot and self-edit these days.' Ruth hoisted the camera onto her other shoulder. 'You weren't expecting a whole crew, were you?'

'Of course not,' said Norah, pulling an 'are you mad?' face. A dull flush crept up her neck. She flicked a speck of dust from her jacket.

'The ponies are all ready,' she said, her composure recovered. 'What do you want to do first - film our routine or interview me?'

Ruth blinked. Kristy had the feeling she didn't meet many thirteen-year-olds as assertive as Norah Bergman.

'Um, the planning editor said I've got to interview the owner of the blind horse.' Ruth consulted a battered notebook. 'Kristy Moore. Is that you?'

Norah shot the reporter a look that could have frozen boiling water. William gave Kristy a gentle shove forwards.

Kristy swallowed. 'It's me. But your planning editor has made a mistake. Cassius isn't blind, he's just lost his sight in one eye.'

'One bad eye is good enough for me,' Ruth said cheerfully. 'It'll still make a nice heartwarming piece for the end of the programme. Where is he?'

Kristy pointed to the Percheron, who was standing patiently outside his stable, pulling wisps of hay from a haynet.

'Big, isn't he?' said Ruth.

'He's small for a Percheron, actually. But plenty big enough for me. Want to say hello?'

'Absolutely,' said Ruth, digging about in the pocket of her coat. 'I bought some Polos especially.'

'He'll love you forever,' grinned Kristy.

'Nothing wrong with a bit of cupboard love. We'll do the interview first, then I'll film you all in action. So you might as well go and get ready,' Ruth told the others, seemingly oblivious to Norah's baleful stare. 'We don't want the other ponies distracting the star of the show, do we?' she added kindly.

'You're right, of course. That would be beyond awful,' said Norah, her voice heavy with sarcasm. Her blonde curls bounced indignantly as she turned on her heels and stomped across the yard to Silver. Kristy winced as Norah yanked down her stirrup leathers, sprang into the saddle and wheeled her plump dappled grey gelding towards the indoor school.

William hooted with laughter. 'About time someone took her down a peg or two.'

He vaulted onto Copper and trotted after his sister. Sofia blew Kristy a kiss and followed. Ruth was on one knee, fiddling with her camera. Kristy leant on Cassius. Suddenly her mouth felt as dry as sandpaper. She swallowed.

'How did your planning editor know about Cassius's eye?'

'It was in the paper. I've got a photocopy in the car somewhere.'

'Of course.' Kristy had forgotten the local paper had run a story about the quadrille in its coverage of the Mayor's New Year's Eve show. The reporter who'd turned up at the stables to interview them had angled his story on the fact that Sofia, William and Norah had pooled their winnings to buy him for Kristy after he'd been abandoned by his old owner.

Ruth lifted the camera back onto her shoulder. 'OK, so I'll just ask you a few questions. All straightforward. Nothing to be worried about.'

Kristy untied Cassius. He gave her a gentle nudge and she plucked an errant wisp of hay from his mane and straightened his forelock. She licked her lips and gave Ruth the ghost of a smile.

'Ready?'

'As I'll ever be.'

'Righto. So, tell me Kristy, how did Cassius come to lose the sight in his eye?'

'He had an eye infection and unfortunately the vet couldn't save his sight.'

'How does it affect him day to day?'

'Horses adapt really well to losing their sight. I always approach him on his good side so he can see me, and I talk to him, so he knows I'm there. Sometimes he can be a bit spooky on his left rein but if I let him stop and look at stuff he's fine.'

'Did it impact on your training for the quadrille?'

'A bit,' Kristy admitted. 'We had to get Cassius used to the others riding past his blind side. But we got there in the end.'

'You certainly did. The Mayor says your routine was the highlight of the show.'

'Cassius had the time of his life,' said Kristy, rubbing the gelding's ear.

'He must trust you.'

Kristy smiled properly for the first time. 'He does. I have to be his eyes, you see. He looks after me and I look after him.'

'And your team-mates clubbed together to buy him for you, I believe?'

Kristy nodded. Sometimes she still couldn't believe Cassius was really hers. 'His old owner abandoned him when he lost his sight because she didn't want to pay the vet's bills. Emma, who's the owner of Mill Farm Stables, needed to sell him to recoup the money. Luckily for me she sold him to us.'

'I wonder if his old owner regrets her decision now.'

Kristy shivered. It was as if someone had thrown a bucket of icy water down her back. Her grip on Cassius's reins tightened.

'I don't know. Probably. Wouldn't you?' She looked at Ruth desperately. 'You won't use that bit, will you?'

Ruth pressed a button on her camera and eased it onto the ground. 'No, I only needed a soundbite. Let's go and film the quadrille.'

For the next half an hour Ruth filmed them as they ran through their routine. She had them vaulting on and off until they were dizzy and made them repeat their serpentines and two-way crossovers until she was happy she had enough footage. Kristy thought she would be able to relax now her interview was over and she was doing what she loved most in the world - riding her beloved Percheron. But she felt anxious. The fluttering in her heart had been replaced by a leaden feeling, an inexplicable sense of dread as if she'd forgotten to hand in a vital piece of homework and was now going to fail all her exams. To make matters worse, Norah kept shooting her filthy looks, and every time she sneaked a peek at Ruth, the camera was trained on Cassius. Kristy had the horrible feeling he was the only reason Ruth was there.

Eventually Ruth called, 'It's a wrap,' and they halted in front of her, their cheeks flushed and the ponies' coats steaming.

'Thanks guys, that was awesome. It'll probably be reduced to two minutes by the time it goes out, but at least it'll be an action-packed two minutes.' Ruth smiled and stretched her back.

Kristy could feel Norah's eyes burning a hole in her back as they led the ponies back to the yard. Suddenly she had an idea. 'Sofia, can you take Cassius a sec? I need to have a quick word with Ruth.'

Not waiting for an answer, she flung her reins at Sofia and ran after Ruth, whispering in her ear. Ruth looked puzzled, glanced at Norah and her face cleared. She nodded and picked up the camera again.

'Hey Norah, don't forget I need a soundbite from you, too,' she called.

'That was a nice thing to do,' said Sofia quietly as they untacked Cassius and Jazz.

Kristy shrugged. 'Norah's much better at this kind of thing than me. And we wouldn't have won the quadrille if she hadn't kept us all in line.'

'Bullied us into behaving you mean,' Sofia giggled.

It wasn't until she was walking home that Kristy realised what had been bugging her. How could Cassius have sneaked into the kitchen if both the back door and the kitchen door were closed? There was a Shetland pony in the book she was reading that could undo quick release knots and bolts on stable doors in the blink of an eye. Maybe Cassius had taught himself how to slip open the bolt on his gate and had decided to go exploring?

Cassius was by far the cleverest horse Kristy had ever met. But even she, his number one fan, thought it was unlikely he'd worked out how to open not one but two doors all by himself.

3

MISS RAVEN'S REQUEST

'Kristy Moore!' boomed a voice across the atrium outside the school hall. Kristy stopped in her tracks. She didn't need to look around to know it was the voice of their head teacher.

The swarm of students heading out of assembly pushed past her, diverging like a fast-flowing river around a lichen-clad boulder. As she tried to turn her rucksack caught the shoulder of a sixth-former.

'Oi, watch where you're going!' he cried, glaring at her.

'Sorry,' Kristy muttered. 'I was just trying to -'

'Kristy Moore!' the voice bellowed again. 'In my office. *Now!*'

Kristy felt a buzz of alarm. What had she done to incur the wrath of Miss Raven? She knew she had a tendency to daydream but she'd worked really hard to get her grades back up to where they should be. She'd had no choice - her parents had told her she'd have to stop working at Mill Farm if they didn't improve. No, it couldn't be that. Mr Baker had given her As for her last two assignments and he was easily the strictest teacher in school. She glanced down involuntarily. Nothing incensed Miss Raven more than school uniform violations. Turned up skirts could earn you a hefty ten behaviour points and forgetting your tie was a serious offence punishable by an after school detention. Rumour had it she'd once expelled a boy who'd dared turn up to school in roller shoes.

But Kristy's uniform was all in order. White shirt, navy jumper, navy and plum tartan pleated skirt and navy tights. She'd even polished her shoes. OK, so her dad had, but Miss Raven needn't know that. The point was they were so clean she could see her worried face reflected back at her.

Kristy took a deep breath and forced her way back through the throng towards the head's office. Miss Raven ushered her in and motioned to a squishy armchair in front of her ornately-carved desk.

'Make yourself comfortable, Kristy. I just need to make a quick phone call.'

Kristy sank into the depths of the armchair and scanned the room. The only other time she'd been in Miss Raven's office was the day she'd visited the school with her parents just before they'd moved. To say she'd been a little in awe of her new head teacher had been an understatement. Miss Raven was a fearsome woman, with cropped pewter-grey hair and piercing blue eyes. When she looked at you, you felt as though you were walking through an X-ray machine at the airport. It was as if she could gaze right into your soul and read your innermost thoughts.

She'd asked Kristy if she'd been worried about leaving her private school to start at the state school on the other side of town. Kristy had shrugged. It wasn't as if she'd had a choice. Since her dad had lost his job a lot had changed. But she loved their cosy apartment, even if her mum still hankered after their big detached house with a view of the hills. If they'd still had plenty of cash to splash she'd never have needed a job at Mill Farm Stables. And she would never have met Cassius.

Changing schools had been harder than she'd thought it would be, and it had taken her a long time to make friends. But now she had Sofia, Norah and William. Life was good.

Kristy realised with horror Miss Raven had finished her phone call and was perched on the corner of her desk looking at her expectantly.

'So, what do you think?'

Kristy twiddled with the pleats of her skirt. 'I'm really sorry, Miss Raven. I didn't...I wasn't...I mean, what did you say?'

The head smiled wryly. 'I heard you were prone to daydreaming, Kristy Moore.'

Kristy blushed.

'I was just explaining how I saw your quadrille team on the local news last night and I was very impressed. I wondered if you'd consider putting together a routine for the school's centenary celebration next month?'

Kristy bit her lip. 'Well, it's not really -'

'It's invite only and you won't be the only students on the bill, if that's what you're worried about. The school choir is singing a couple of numbers, Mrs Brown's gymnastic's squad is taking part, and the drama club is re-enacting a day in the life of the school a hundred years ago.'

'It's not that. The thing is, it's not my team. Norah's in charge.'

'Norah Bergman in 9C?'

Kristy nodded. 'It's just she gets a bit -' she fished around for the right word. 'A bit *sensitive* when people assume I'm the leader, just because of Cassius. He's my horse,' she added.

Miss Raven steepled her fingers. 'I see. So it would be

more...diplomatic, shall we say... if I asked Norah and not you?'

Kristy bobbed her head vigorously. 'Yes, Miss Raven. It absolutely would.'

≈

WHEN WILLIAM PASSED her a note in chemistry and Kristy saw two words in Norah's hastily-scribbled writing - *Library lunchtime!* - she knew Miss Raven had been as good as her word.

The bell for lunch was still ringing in her ears as she pushed open the door of the library. Norah was already sitting at their usual table, fidgeting in her chair like a cat on hot bricks.

Kristy slid into the seat next to her. 'What's up?'

'Amazing news!' Norah whispered.

Kristy nudged her. 'Spill the beans, then.'

'I can't tell you until the others are here.' Norah drummed her fingers on the table. 'Where *are* they?'

William arrived next, followed by Sofia, who was looking around her distractedly.

'You haven't seen my PE kit, have you?' she said.

'Er, why would we?' said William.

'You're hopeless,' said Kristy. 'Where did you last see it?'

'Never mind that now,' Norah hissed. 'I've got something to tell you. Miss Raven came to find me after geography. You'll never guess what she wanted.'

'To make you head girl because you're easily the bossiest girl in the school?' said William.

Norah shook her head impatiently. 'You're being ridiculous. She only wants us to perform a quadrille in the school's centenary celebration!' She beamed at them all.

Kristy acted surprised. 'You're kidding?'

'No, I'm not. She saw us on the telly and thought we were brilliant.'

'That's awesome!' cried Sofia, her lost PE bag forgotten.

'Fantastic!' said Kristy, sending silent thanks to Miss Raven.

'Is that it?' said William, pushing back his chair. 'I'm outta here. Time and tide and football wait for no man, you know.'

Norah glowered at his retreating back. 'Sometimes I don't think he's on the same planet as us.'

'Mars,' said Kristy wisely.

'What?'

'You know the saying. Men are from Mars and women are from Venus. Different planets, like you said.'

'Right,' said Norah, but Kristy could tell she wasn't listening. 'Who cares what he thinks anyway. I've been planning some new moves we can incorporate in the routine. Half-passes and maybe even some flying changes. What d'you reckon?'

'Maybe we shouldn't be too ambitious. Better to perform a faultless simple routine than mess up a complicated one,' said Sofia.

But Norah had the faraway look in her eye Kristy recognised only too well, and she knew it was only a matter of time before she handed them all colour co-ordinated folders containing diagrams so complicated they made IKEA flat-pack instructions look like child's play.

～

IT'S FUNNY, Kristy mused, as she led Cassius into the yard. He hadn't escaped from his paddock once since the day Ruth had filmed them. She tied him up outside his stable, slipping the end of his lead rope through the loop in the quick release knot just in case he decided to practice his newfound escape artist skills while she fetched his grooming kit.

She'd raced through evening stables so she would have time for a quick schooling session before she went home. Norah's hankering to include half-passes and flying changes in their routine had made her heart sink. Although Cassius was far more supple than he'd ever been, they hadn't tried any lateral work.

'How can I give you the correct aids when I don't even know what a half-pass is supposed to look like?' she said, leading him over to the mounting block. As they rode into the indoor school one of the strip lights flickered and died.

Remembering Sofia's comment Kristy decided to stick to simple circles and serpentines and soon she was totally absorbed, making sure Cassius was balanced and working in an outline. She didn't notice Emma slip into the school until she eased the Percheron into a walk and let the reins slip through her fingers so he could stretch his neck.

'He's looking great,' the older woman said approvingly. 'You work well together.'

Kristy glowed with pleasure. Emma didn't hand out compliments often and when she did Kristy savoured them.

She ran a hand down Cassius's neck and jumped off. They meandered back to the yard.

'Emma, what is lateral work?'

'It's when you ask a horse to move forwards and sideways at the same time.'

'So what's the difference between a leg yield, a half-pass and a shoulder-in?'

Emma made a show of glancing at her watch. 'How long have you got?'

Kristy's shoulders slumped. 'It's complicated, then.'

Emma smiled. 'It's not something I can explain in five

minutes, no.' She thought for a minute. 'Are you doing anything Sunday morning?'

Sunday was Kristy's one day off at Mill Farm Stables.

'I was going to hack out with the others, that's all. We're meeting at ten.'

'Tell you what, if you're here at nine come and find me. It's easier to explain if I show you.'

4

BLUE LIGHTS

*W*hen Kristy pedalled into the yard at ten to nine on Sunday morning Emma was tacking up her big skewbald gelding, Jigsaw.

'We used to do quite a bit of dressage, back in the day,' said Emma, lengthening her stirrup leathers. 'We're a bit rusty, but we should be able to manage a bit of lateral work, shouldn't we, my old friend?' She gave the skewbald a brisk pat.

As she followed Emma and Jigsaw into the school, Kristy remembered the flickering strip light.

'I forgot to tell you yesterday. One of the bulbs has blown,' she said, pointing to the offending light.

'I know. One of the liveries mentioned it, too. It's top of my to do list.'

Kristy stood in the middle of the school, her hands deep in her pockets, and watched Emma circle the gelding at a walk and trot.

'So, as I explained the other day, lateral work is when you ask the horse to move at an angle,' said Emma, bringing

Jigsaw back to a walk. Their transitions were as smooth as silk.

'When it's done properly, lateral work develops the horse's muscles and balance and improves his suppleness. Think of it as equine gymnastics,' Emma continued, changing diagonal and riding Jigsaw on the left rein.

She turned off the track just before C, along the three quarter line. 'This is a leg yield. See, Jigsaw's head is flexed slightly away from the direction of travel and his body is straight. See how his inside leg crosses over in front of his outside leg as he makes his way to the rails?'

Kristy was mesmerised. 'How do you get him to do that?'

'My left leg is behind the girth asking him to move sideways towards the edge of the school and my left rein is asking for a small amount of flexion. I'm using my right rein to control his shoulders and my right leg is on the girth to maintain forward momentum and to stop him falling out. Good lad!' she said breathlessly as they reached the end of the school.

She changed rein again and talked Kristy through a leg yield on the right leg before bringing Jigsaw back to a walk.

'I think I get it,' said Kristy. 'So what's a half-pass?'

'That's more difficult to master. In half-pass, the horse's body is bent *towards* the direction of travel. But you really need to master the shoulder-in first.'

Kristy's brain felt as scrambled as the eggs she'd had on her toast for breakfast. 'And a shoulder-in?' she said faintly.

Emma chuckled. 'It's a lot to take in, isn't it? For a shoulder in the horse should be bent around a rider's inside leg so the horse's inside hind leg and outside foreleg travel on the same line. Why do you want to know all this, anyway?'

Kristy told her about Norah's plans for their school's centenary celebration.

'I'd love to learn all this, I really would. But the centenary's only a few weeks away. There's no way we'll nail it by then,' said Kristy.

'I'm inclined to agree. I admire Norah for being so ambitious but she needs to be realistic. Leave it with me. I'll have a word with her.'

∼

THEIR SUNDAY MORNING hack was the highlight of Kristy's week. Weekdays were hectic as she squeezed school, homework and her job at the stables into days that just weren't long enough. She worked at Mill Farm from nine to three every Saturday and if she didn't go straight home her mum started muttering about her spending more time with the horses than she did with them.

But Sundays were sacrosanct. She lay in until half past seven - what luxury! - and had a leisurely breakfast before cycling over to the stables by nine o'clock so she had time to give Cassius's tack a quick clean before she caught him and groomed him.

If she had time to ride in the week she was lucky if she spent more than ten minutes cleaning off the worst of the mud. But on Sundays Kristy groomed the Percheron from the tip of his smoky black ears to the bottom of his wavy tail, brushing his coat until it shone and oiling his hooves.

The four children took it in turns to choose a route then they disappeared for hours along the bridleways and lanes surrounding Mill Farm Stables. They rode in all weathers, from days when the ground was crisp with frost and their fingers and toes froze, to drizzly mornings when diaphanous rain coated their eyelashes with tiny beads of water. The only time they cancelled was in howling wind and horizontal rain.

'Who's choosing?' said William, vaulting nimbly onto Copper's back. Since the New Year's Eve show he hadn't been near the mounting block, choosing to hone his vaulting skills instead.

'Me,' said Sofia. 'Sproggett's Farm today, I think.'

Kristy grinned. It was her favourite ride, too. The route took them down pretty country lanes where, if they were lucky, buzzards wheeled overhead, into woodland. Then there was a long gallop along the side of an arable field before they passed Sproggett's Farm and turned for home.

Emma appeared from the barn, a stepladder under her arm. 'Have a good ride!' she called.

'We will,' they chorused back.

The sun was shining in a bleached-blue sky and catkins hung from branches like tiny lambs' tails. Spring was definitely just around the corner. Kristy slotted into her normal place next to Sofia and Jazz and they chatted about their week while the twins bickered amicably behind them.

Cassius could obviously smell spring in the air, too. He walked with a bounce to his stride, his ears pricked as he looked around him with his good eye.

'He looks a million dollars,' said Sofia.

'That's what Emma said.' Kristy played with a hank of his mane and smiled down at Sofia. Secretly she loved the fact Cassius towered over the other ponies.

'I bet his old owner wouldn't recognise him,' Sofia continued.

The smile slid from Kristy's face. She didn't like to be reminded that Cassius had been anyone's except hers.

Two hours later they clip-clopped along the lane at the back of the stables. It had been an idyllic ride. The ponies and Cassius had behaved impeccably, the sun had felt warm on their backs and the twins hadn't murdered each other.

Cassius stopped metres from the back gate, planting all four feet firmly on the asphalt. Kristy clicked her tongue. 'Come on, Cass. Nearly home.'

But the black gelding wouldn't take another step. His head shot up and he sniffed the wind with quivering nostrils. The ponies, picking up on his alarm, fidgeted on the spot.

'What's up?' said Sofia, trying to calm a panicky Jazz.

'No idea.' Kristy kicked Cassius on but the Percheron, normally so willing, still wouldn't budge. Kristy felt his body tremble as he gave a high-pitched whinny. She slid off and rubbed his blaze.

'It's alright, kiddo. There's nothing to be frightened of, I promise.'

He lowered his head a fraction and she scratched his poll. 'There you are, see? I'll look after you.'

She clicked her tongue again and Cassius followed her reluctantly down the lane towards the gate. Kristy let the others through and closed it with a click.

'I can hear something now,' said William suddenly. 'It sounds like a siren.'

Sure enough, the unmistakable wail of a siren cut through the air.

'Perhaps there's been a robbery!' said William.

'Don't be stupid,' said Norah. 'What would they steal, pony nuts?'

The siren stopped and the four children looked at each other.

'I hope there hasn't been an accident.' Kristy tugged Cassius's reins and ran up the track that led past his paddock to the stable yard, the Percheron trotting obediently behind her.

She heard the low rumble of a diesel engine and saw blue lights reflected in a puddle of water outside the barn before she'd even turned the corner into the yard. She flung her reins at Sofia and sprinted towards the sound, her heart in her mouth.

5

SLAVE LABOUR

*K*risty skidded to a halt. Two paramedics in forest-green shirts and cargo trousers were lifting a stretcher into the back of an ambulance. Kristy recognised the boots poking out from under the blanket immediately.

'Emma!' she cried, crossing the yard in a couple of strides.

Emma's face was as white as wax and her eyes were slightly glazed, like an out-of-focus photograph.

Kristy peered at her anxiously. 'What's happened?'

'She's broken her arm. Fell off a stepladder,' said the older of the paramedics. He placed a mask over Emma's face and gave her a reassuring smile. 'Gas and air. For the pain. Don't worry, we'll soon have you in hospital.'

Emma breathed in deeply and at once Kristy could see some of the tension leave her face. After a couple more deep breaths she took the mask from her face with her good hand.

'Kristy, you need to phone Karen. Tell her what's happened.'

'Karen?' Kristy couldn't disguise her surprise. It was

common knowledge Emma and her younger sister didn't get on.

Emma grimaced and took another deep lungful of gas and air. 'Yes, Karen. Tell her she needs to get her backside over here pronto.'

Emma must have noticed the look of alarm on Kristy's face as her mouth twitched. 'On second thoughts, don't put it quite so bluntly. Ask her very nicely if she would look after the horses while I'm in hospital. Remind her she owes me for the time I looked after Coldblow for two weeks when she had her appendix out. Tell her I'll be back in the morning.'

'I'm not sure you will be,' said the paramedic. 'I reckon they'll keep you in for at least a couple of days. It looks like a nasty break to me.'

Emma shook her head. The movement made her wince. She clutched Kristy's hand. 'Don't tell her that, whatever you do.'

Kristy glanced over her shoulder. The others were standing a few metres away, shocked into silence.

'There's no need to ask Karen. We can look after the yard. I know what to do,' she said in a rush.

'I know you do, Kristy. But I have to have an adult in charge for the insurance. What if something happens and I'm not covered? I can't take the risk.' Emma's voice was flat. 'We have no choice. We have to ask my baby sister.'

∾

THE STACCATO SOUND of a car door slamming made Kristy's heart sink. She had been mindlessly stuffing hay into haynets in the barn while the others changed rugs and filled water buckets. She dropped the haynet she was filling and trudged into the yard.

The phone call to Karen had gone as well as she had predicted.

'She wants *what?*' Karen had barked so loudly Kristy had snatched the phone away from her ear.

'Just twenty four hours, Emma said. And,' Kristy had taken a deep breath, 'she said to remind you of the fortnight she helped you out after your operation.'

'I bet she did,' said Karen nastily.

'Sorry. I did offer to do it,' said Kristy in a small voice.

Her apology was met with silence. Kristy was beginning to wonder if Karen had hung up on her when there was a loud exclamation of breath.

'I suppose I don't have a choice. I'll be over at four. You'll have to make do without me until then.'

Kristy had filled in the others over a hot chocolate in the tack room.

'She's got a nerve,' William huffed.

'She has got her own riding stables to run,' said Norah. Kristy remembered how impressed Norah had been when they'd recced Coldblow before the New Year's Eve show.

'She told us she's got three other instructors, remember. Emma's a one man band,' said Sofia.

'She has me, too. And I owe it to her to make sure there's not a wisp of hay out of place when Karen arrives.' Kristy drained her mug and stood up. She had thirteen horses to look after. She'd already told her parents she wouldn't be home until at least six.

Sofia also jumped to her feet. 'I'll help. Anything to get me out of my history homework.'

'We'll help, too, won't we Norah?' said William.

Norah took their mugs. 'I don't mind doing Silver because he's my pony. But I don't get paid to muck out the others. Kristy does.'

'Norah!' said Sofia. 'Not on a Sunday she doesn't. And

anyway, we're doing this for Emma, not for Kristy. Emma works all day every day looking after our ponies. Helping her now is the least we can do.'

Kristy felt like hugging Sofia and was glad to see Norah had the grace to look a little shamefaced.

They divvied up the jobs and set to work. By three o'clock the thirteen stables had been mucked out and the paddocks had been poo-picked. Norah, who was complaining bitterly of an aching back and blistered hands, was tasked with mixing the evening feeds, following the set of instructions tacked to the wall of the feed room. William swept the yard with the yard brush he had used as a substitute pony when Copper was lame the previous winter. Sofia and Kristy brought in Cassius, Jigsaw and Mill Farm's eleven liveries.

Kristy leant against Cassius's stable door and the Percheron blew softly into her neck as she surveyed the yard.

'I'd say that was a job well done,' she said with satisfaction.

'But it's not exactly Coldblow, is it?' said Sofia glumly.

Kristy pictured Karen's magazine-perfect yard, where stablehands were bawled out if so much as a twist of shavings was out of place. At Mill Farm the concrete was crumbling in places and everything needed a lick of paint.

'It isn't,' Kristy agreed. She snaked her arm around Cassius's neck and lay her face against his cheek. 'But at least the horses are happy.'

~

KAREN STOOD beside her gleaming white Land Rover Sport with her hands on her hips and her mouth turned down. She consulted her mobile phone.

'Which one of you is Emma's stablehand?'

Kristy yelped as Norah gave her a shove in the back.

'Me,' she said reluctantly.

'I've spoken to the hospital. She's going to be in for at least four days.'

Kristy widened her eyes and crossed her fingers behind her back. 'Is she?' she squeaked.

'So much for twenty four hours. So we need to get a few ground rules straight. I'm here in a supervisory capacity only. I won't be getting my hands dirty. I presume you've finished evening stables?'

'Yes, it's all done.'

'Well, that's something, I suppose.' Karen waved an arm at the boot of the Land Rover. 'Perhaps you'd bring my luggage to the house.'

She stalked off towards the back door.

'What did her last slave die of?' William grumbled.

Kristy shrugged, opened the boot and reached for the matching suitcase and travel bag inside.

'What are you doing that for?' whispered Sofia. 'She's not your boss.'

'I think it was a rhetorical question,' said Kristy. 'And anyway, she technically is. For the next few days anyway.'

'Good luck with that,' said William. 'Come on Norah, we told Mum we'd be home by half four. He blew his unruly fringe out of his eyes. 'See you at school.'

Kristy watched her three friends disappear down the driveway. She picked up the bags and trudged into the house.

Karen was in the kitchen, staring at the sink full of dirty crockery with a look of undisguised disdain.

'I see my sister still lives by the same code as she always has.'

'Code?'

'Horses before housework.' Karen picked up a yellow dishcloth with her thumb and forefinger and held it at arm's length. She sniffed it gingerly and dropped it back onto the draining board with a shudder.

'I suppose she hadn't planned to break her arm today,' said Kristy reasonably.

Karen gave her a tight smile. 'I suppose not. Perhaps when you've carried my bags up to the spare room you'd like to wash up.'

It was another of those rhetorical questions, Kristy thought as she lugged Karen's two bags up the stairs and along the landing to the biggest of Emma's spare rooms. She must be so used to giving orders at Coldblow she'd forgotten how to ask nicely.

Karen was staring moodily at a collage of photos pinned to the cork board on the back of the kitchen door when Kristy reappeared.

'I've made up the bed. And found you a couple of clean towels.'

Karen pointed to a photo in the centre of the board and stared at her appraisingly. 'Was that you riding Arabella Hayward's Percheron in the quadrille?'

'I rode Cassius, yes. But he doesn't belong to Arabella Hayward. He's mine. I don't even know who she is.'

'She owns him. At least she used to. She used to box him over from Emma's to Coldblow for lessons with me. Nice horse. I'm surprised she sold him.'

Kristy felt a tiny twist of fear deep in her stomach. She bent her head over the washing up bowl so Karen couldn't see her face.

'She didn't sell him. She abandoned him,' she mumbled.

'I wouldn't throw around allegations like that if I were you.'

Kristy picked up a saucepan and scrubbed at the congealed pasta sauce stuck to the bottom. 'She did. She owed Emma six months in livery fees and a small fortune to the vet. Emma kept him in lieu of the money she was owed, and my friends clubbed together to buy him for me with their winnings from the quadrille.' She dropped the pan on the draining board with a clatter.

Karen sucked her teeth. 'That's rather...unorthodox.'

Kristy swirled foamy water inside a tumbler. 'So what do you do when someone doesn't pay you?'

'Take them to the small claims court, of course.' Karen pointed a long-nailed index finger at a piece of dried tomato still stuck to the bottom of the saucepan. 'You've missed a bit.'

6

CALLING THE SHOTS

'She's an absolute nightmare. All she does is order me about and then pick faults if my work isn't perfect.' Kristy slumped over her schoolbag. She knew she was being a drama queen but honestly, the others had no idea.

'I got an earful last night because I left the tap running while I nipped into Copper's stable to get his water bucket. OK so it made a small puddle. But it was hardly the Niagara Falls!'

Norah, who had summoned them to the library at morning break to hand out the new routine, tutted. But if Kristy thought she, too, disapproved of Karen's exacting ways she was wrong.

'She just has high standards. Think of it as valuable work experience. You'll know what it's like to work in a high-end yard. Let's face it, Coldblow is a cut above Mill Farm.'

Indignation rose like bile in Kristy's throat.

'If you think she's so great, perhaps you'd like to -'

'At last!' Norah said, as Sofia pushed open the library door, followed closely by William.

Kristy bit her lip. She hadn't finished with Norah, but for now it would have to wait.

Once Sofia and William had settled opposite them, Norah pulled out four sheets of laminated paper from her bag. She flexed one experimentally.

'I've laminated them so we can take them down to the stables and they won't get ruined.' She handed three to Kristy. 'Take one and hand them round,' she said bossily.

Kristy raised her eyebrows but did as she was told.

'Initially, as you know, I was planning to move it up a gear and introduce some more advanced moves. Half-passes and flying changes, you know the sort of thing. But I had a long chat with Emma before she broke her arm, and she said we'd be better off perfectly executing a simple routine than mucking up a more complex one.'

'Actually, that's what I said,' said Sofia.

Norah ignored her. 'I've left out the vaulting -'

'There's a surprise,' William muttered. Vaulting wasn't Norah's strong point.

'But I have introduced some new moves and we're going to do some canter work, which should look really impressive.' She looked at them all down her freckly nose. '*If* we get it right. So, please memorise the routine before our first practice ride at six tonight.'

'Aren't we having a walk-through first?' Kristy was surprised. They'd walked their routine for the New Year's Eve show several times before they'd tried riding it.

Norah waved her hand dismissively. 'No time. We've only got a couple of weeks. It'll be fine. As long as you've remembered it,' she smiled thinly.

It was only as they reached the atrium, about to go their separate ways, that Sofia clutched Norah's arm.

'What about the music? The costumes?'

'Don't panic, it's all sorted,' said Norah serenely. 'I've

chosen a different piece of music by the same composer we used last time. It's the perfect tempo. And we're going to wear school uniform from the turn of the century. Pinafores and straw boaters -'

'I am *not* wearing a pinafore!' William exploded. A couple of Year Sevens loitering in front of the school hall nudged each other and giggled.

Norah shook her head. 'If you'd just let me finish. Pinafores and boaters for the girls and shorts, a knitted tank top and a flat cap for you.'

Kristy felt anger flare inside her, like the flame of a candle caught in a draught of wind. 'Seems like you've thought of everything. I'm amazed you even need us.'

Doubt clouded Norah's face. 'What do you mean?'

'We're a team, remember? You might be in charge, but sometimes it would be nice if you asked us before you decided what we're doing.'

'You know me.' Norah attempted a smile. 'I can't help myself.'

Kristy swung her bag onto her shoulder. 'Then maybe you should try.'

Kristy sat at the back of the classroom, her chin cupped in one hand, and stared moodily out of the window. By the whiteboard their history teacher, Mr Petersen, was intoning the causes of the Second World War. Kristy let his words drift over her like wisps of cirrus cloud as she silently fumed. Once again Norah was calling all the shots. She was a human steamroller. Her way was the only way. William may make a show of standing up to his sister, but when push came to shove he always deferred to her. Sofia was too nice to argue with her. Usually Kristy let Norah have her way. Anything for a quiet life. But she'd had enough. She pictured herself stomping up to Norah at the stables and letting rip. Norah would be contrite for once in her life, telling her meekly that she could lead the team. Kristy slid down her chair and imagined the fun she'd have, bossing Norah about for a change.

Slowly she became aware of a dozen pairs of eyes swivelling in her direction. At the forefront of them was Mr Petersen, his eyes narrowed over his half-moon spectacles. Kristy wriggled surreptitiously back up the chair and picked up her fountain pen, as poised as a shorthand secretary.

'Perhaps you'd like to share with us your thoughts on the Treaty of Versailles?' said the history teacher with a smile that stopped at his cheekbones.

Kristy cleared her throat, tapped her pen on her chin in what she hoped was an authoritative manner, and stole a glance at the open textbook in front of her.

'Um. Well. I suppose if Hitler hadn't resented the restrictions forced on Germany by the rest of Europe he might not have been so keen to expand his empire and invade Austria. That could be a thing, couldn't it?' she finished lamely.

Mr Petersen nodded curtly. 'Yes, that could indeed be a thing.'

Kristy gave a silent sigh of relief as the teacher pointed his ruler at a sullen-looking boy called Edward on the other side of the classroom and asked him to define reparation. She must stop daydreaming. She had dodged a bullet this time, but if she ended up with a lunchtime detention she'd never have a chance to learn their new routine before their practice. She needed to have it down to a tee. There was no way she was giving Norah another opportunity to patronise her.

At lunchtime Kristy found a quiet corner near the netball courts and pulled the laminated routine out of her rucksack.

Like before, it was a complicated mass of arrows and squiggles, but at least this time she could picture each section in her mind's eye.

She had to admit it was a triumph. Norah had played to their strengths, keeping the movements to simple circles and changes of the diagonal. She had them weaving in and out of each other like bobbins making lace. It would be mesmerising to watch. And fiendishly difficult to remember.

Kristy stared at the plan until her eyes went blurry, tracing her set of arrows with her index finger, imagining Cassius's pricked ears and steady stride as they looped and spiralled in the school. By the time the bell went for afternoon lessons she had mastered most of the routine. She pulled herself to her feet, massaging her cramped shins, and set off for the science labs. She had to be at Mill Farm by four o'clock. She didn't have any spare time to cram the final few moves. It would have to do.

~

KAREN'S immaculate Land Rover was nowhere to be seen when Kristy sprinted up the Mill Farm drive. At least she'd be able to finish evening stables without her temporary boss breathing down her neck. She made a beeline for the wheelbarrow and wheeled it straight over to Jazz's stable.

When Kristy had first started working at the livery yard she'd only been responsible for looking after Silver, Copper and Jazz. Mucking out their three stables, bringing them in, changing their rugs and feeding them had taken every second of her two hour shift.

But the longer she'd worked at Mill Farm the quicker she'd become. She'd developed all manner of time-saving strategies so she could whizz through her jobs and still have time to spend with Cassius.

Kristy made up a week's worth of haynets on a Saturday to save time in the week. She brushed baby oil into the ponies' tails so mud and dust didn't stick, saving her precious minutes when she groomed them. She never carried one bucket, or led in one pony, when she could manage two.

She watched Emma like a hawk, noting how efficiently her boss worked. Emma didn't get distracted when Marmalade, the ginger stable cat, came weaving around her legs wanting a fuss or when a brown-flecked buzzard decided to use the top of the nearest telegraph pole as a vantage point. There was no time for daydreaming if she wanted to spend twenty minutes grooming Cassius or snatch a quick half hour ride in the school before she was expected home for dinner.

As she'd become faster, Emma had given her more jobs and these days, as well as looking after the ponies, she mucked out three of the other liveries and mixed feeds for the whole yard. Handling the bigger horses like Viking, the handsome bay warmblood who shared a paddock with Emma's horse Jigsaw, was second nature.

So she hadn't been too fazed when she realised she was going to be responsible for all thirteen horses while Emma was in hospital. She'd sat down with a pen and paper and listed all the essential jobs, and those that could wait until she had more time. She'd taken an executive decision to deep litter all the beds. Extras like tack-cleaning and rug washing could also wait. Once they'd heard about the accident a couple of the long-standing owners had offered to muck out their own horses until Emma was back on her feet and Kristy had accepted their help gratefully. Sofia had promised she'd spend Saturday helping her catch up with all the jobs she'd had to leave during the week. Between them they would get it done.

Kristy was picking out Viking's feet when she heard the

guttural sound of a car engine. Expecting to see Karen's Land Rover swing into the yard she dropped the hoof pick in surprise as a red sports car spun in, stopping with a tyre squeal outside the barn.

Viking skittered sideways like a flustered ballerina and Kristy ran her hand down his neck to soothe him.

'It's OK, kiddo. It's just some idiot driver with no manners.' A memory tugged at her consciousness and she glared at the man climbing out of the car. 'The same idiot driver who covered me with mud the day Ruth came to film us. I hope he's not planning to keep a horse here. Can you imagine?'

Still muttering under her breath, Kristy studiously ignored the interloper and continued to pick out Viking's feet, taking twice as long as she normally did so she wouldn't have to acknowledge him.

Unperturbed, the man strode over and in a haughty voice demanded, 'Where is Miss Miller?'

7

SPORTS CAR MAN

*P*laying for time, Kristy untied Viking and led him into his stable. 'Which one?' she said over her shoulder.

Sports Car Man whipped off his mirrored sunglasses to reveal pale blue eyes. Kristy realised with a start he wasn't as old as she'd first thought. Probably in his early twenties at most. His arrogant manner made him seem much older.

'The proprietor, of course. The one who runs this place.' He swept a derisory hand over the yard, clearly unimpressed by what he saw.

Kristy straightened her back and said coolly, 'Miss *Emma* Miller is in hospital. Miss *Karen* Miller is looking after Mill Farm while Miss *Emma* Miller is -' she fished around for the right words, '- temporarily incapacitated.'

'And where is Miss *Karen* Miller?' said the man, rubbing his nose.

'I expect she's over at her own yard. But I'm sure she'll be back soon.'

The man made an impatient tsk noise and then sneezed

violently. He whisked a monogrammed handkerchief out of his jeans pocket, muttering something about anti-histamines.

Kristy realised that if he was a prospective owner she should probably be more helpful. Emma couldn't afford to turn new business away. 'Can I pass her a message?' she asked grudgingly.

He gave an impatient shake of his head. 'I'll come back tonight.' His pale eyes swept over the yard, lingering on Henry the Friesian, who was watching them over his stable door.

'Is that Cassius?'

'Cassius?' said Kristy, unable to disguise her surprise. 'How do you know Cassius?'

Sports Car Man nodded to himself. 'She's right. He is a handsome fellow.' He turned abruptly. 'Tell Miss Miller I'll be back later.'

He sauntered over to his car. Kristy scuttled after him.

'How do you know Cassius?' she repeated, her voice as reedy as panpipes.

But Sports Car Man either didn't hear or chose not to answer. And as Kristy watched him accelerate away a knot of anxiety tightened in her belly. What if her ruined jodhpurs had indeed been a bad omen, a portent of disaster? Emma had broken her arm, Kristy had been landed with Karen. Everyone knew these things ran in threes. What new catastrophe lay in wait for her?

~

QUESTIONS ABOUT SPORTS Car Man and his motives buzzed around Kristy's head like a niggling cloud of mosquitoes as she finished evening stables. Who was he? Why had he come to see Emma not once but twice in the space of a few days? And, most importantly, how did he know Cassius? Kristy corrected herself. He obviously didn't know Cassius. Anyone who knew anything about horses knew the difference between a Percheron and a Friesian. But he knew there was a black horse called Cassius at Mill Farm Stables.

The arrival of the twins and Sofia jolted her out of her thoughts and, after checking the red convertible had definitely disappeared, she hooked Cassius's headcollar over her shoulder and set off for his paddock.

He was waiting for her, as he so often was, his chin resting on the gate and his ears pricked. His head was bent slightly to the right so he could watch her with his good eye as she skidded down the uneven track. He whickered and she kissed his nose, his whiskers tickling her cheek.

'Hello, beautiful,' she said softly. 'Missed me?'

Cassius nuzzled her neck, nibbling at a strand of hair that had escaped her ponytail.

'I'll take that as a yes.' Kristy fastened his headcollar and led him through the gate. Cassius pulled her towards the patch of long grass on the other side of his fence. Usually she let him graze for a few minutes, but there was no time tonight.

'Sorry, Cass, we have to go or Norah'll be on the warpath again.'

The Percheron sighed loudly. Kristy scratched his ear. 'I'll let you have some when we're finished. Promise.'

Apparently satisfied he wouldn't miss out, Cassius followed Kristy up to the yard. The others were already in the indoor school. Kristy flicked a brush over him, picked out his feet and tacked him up in record time. She rammed her hat on and led him over to the mounting block.

'KRISTEEE!' Norah's voice ricocheted off the stable walls, as loud as a tannoy.

'Just coming!' Kristy yelled back. She tightened Cassius's girth, pulled down his stirrups and jumped on. The flutter of elation she always felt when she rode Cassius fizzed like static down her spine and she smiled, all thoughts of Sports Car Man forgotten.

'Come on, kiddo. Let's show them how it's done.'

It was only as they clattered across the yard towards the open doors of the indoor school and Kristy tried to remember the opening moves that she realised her mind had gone completely blank. The routine she'd tried so hard to learn had evaporated, like vapour trails from a long-departed aeroplane.

8

CIRCLES AND SERPENTINES

She needn't have worried. It soon became clear William hadn't bothered to so much as look at the routine and Sofia, who'd had violin practice at lunchtime and a netball match straight after school, had only had time for one quick read-through.

Norah was – for once – keeping a lid on her impatience. Instead, Kristy noted wryly, she was in patronising mode. Norah the Slightly Superior, always keen to pass on her expert knowledge and skills to her three minions.

'I'll talk us through the routine, shall I? And I think we'd better walk it to start with. Seeing as it's a bit more intricate than the last one.'

The other three nodded obediently. Norah beamed.

'Perfect. So, if you remember, we ride up the centre line two abreast and take the salute. Me and Sofia. William and Kristy.' The three ponies and Cassius shuffled into place and plodded up the centre line.

'Now for our first new move. The scissors.'

'The what?' said William.

'It's a figure of eight, really,' said Kristy, suddenly remembering the second diagram in Norah's routine.

'That's right. When we reach C William and I peel off to the right and Kristy follows Sofia to the left. We thread the needle at X and then we pass each other at A, me and William on the outside and Sofia and Kristy on the inside. Then we ride up each respective side and cross the diagonal again at X. This is all at a trot. With me so far?'

Kristy and the others nodded.

Norah pointed to the door of the school. 'William and I stay on the left rein and canter at A. Sofia and Kristy stay on the left rein and canter at C. We canter a complete circle and at F and H respectively slow to a trot where we cross on the diagonal and each change reins.'

Cassius's ears were pricked, as if he was listening intently to Norah's instructions. Kristy ran a hand down his neck.

'This time we canter on the right rein. William and I start cantering at H. Sofia and Kristy start cantering at F. We both canter complete circles. In fact, it's a circle and a half. When we reach X we come back down to a trot and change the rein before riding the outside track to A. This is where it gets a bit complicated.'

'You mean that wasn't?' said William, his face puckered in concentration.

'Sofia and I pair up again, and William and Kristy follow us up the centre line. We then turn off in opposite directions to do ten metre circles at the same time.'

'I don't understand,' said Sofia. But Kristy could picture them peeling off in opposite directions, Norah and Sofia at G, and her and William at D. She would need to keep Cassius collected otherwise his long strides would overtake Copper, but if they pulled it off it would look pretty impressive.

'You will. Watch,' said Norah, clicking her tongue. Silver

grunted, gave a lazy flick of his tail and walked in a small circle. 'Just imagine we're mirror images of each other.'

Sofia's face cleared. 'I get it. Nice one.'

Norah smiled modestly. 'That's not all. Once we're all back on the centre line heading for C you all follow me onto the right rein and we ride a serpentine down the school. When we're in line with A we ride a windscreen wiper back up again.'

'A windscreen wiper? What on earth is that?' said William.

'If you'd done your homework you wouldn't need to ask,' Norah scolded. 'Imagine a wavy line hitting F, E, M and C. We're riding four abreast so we have to work really hard to keep in line, extending and collecting our trots as necessary. We do one more sweep from H to B where we drop back into pairs and ride back up the centre line to take the final salute.'

'Neat,' said Sofia.

'Pity there isn't any vaulting,' said William.

'Kristy?' Norah looked at her expectantly, her fingers playing with a strand of Silver's mane.

'Yeah, it'll do the job,' said Kristy, feeling a bramble-sharp prickle of shame as Norah's face fell. Contrite, she forced a smile. 'I'm sure Miss Raven will be impressed, anyway.'

Norah nodded, her dignity restored. 'We'll try it at a trot then, shall we?'

~

THE SESSION HAD GONE WELL, Kristy reflected as she ambled home. They'd ridden the routine twice more, and although their circles were uneven and their serpentine more worm than serpent, it was a solid start.

To Kristy's surprise, Karen had appeared halfway through

their final run-through, staying to watch them finish. Norah had flushed with pleasure when she had given a curt nod of approval as they'd filed out of the school.

Praise indeed, thought Kristy, as she'd hung from Cassius's stable door watching him demolish his supper. He'd been a star, listening to her aids, extending and collecting his trot the second she asked. All the hours they'd spent schooling as winter faded into spring had paid off. He was balanced and responsive - a joy to ride.

Kristy's head was so full of serpentines, circles and rein changes as she mooched along the pavement towards home she didn't notice the red sports car pull out of a junction ahead and growl past her, heading inexorably for Mill Farm Stables.

If she had glanced up for even a second she would have seen Sports Car Man in the driving seat. He had one hand on the steering wheel and the other thrown possessively around a girl sitting in the passenger seat beside him. A girl with slash-red lips, long blonde hair as bouncy as a shampoo commercial and a giant diamond gleaming like the North Star on the third finger of her elegant left hand.

If Kristy hadn't been daydreaming about the quadrille she might have wondered why on earth such a glamorous girl was heading for the indisputably shabby Mill Farm Stables.

The sports car's powerful engine growled as it accelerated up the drive, flinging gravel in its wake like sea spray from a speedboat. A magpie, pecking about in the verge, took fright, its black and white wings a blur as it soared over Kristy's head.

It was the bird's angry chatter that finally snapped Kristy out of her daydream, and she looked around, wondering what had startled him.

But the sports car and its occupants had long gone.

9

GONE

Kristy woke just after midnight with a thudding heart and an inexplicable feeling of foreboding. She curled in a ball under her duvet and squeezed her eyes shut. But sleep evaded her, and as she tossed and turned the sense of unease grew.

She must have had a nightmare. As she tried to remember, images spooled in her head, like random pictures on an old cine film. Emma lying on the ground clutching her useless arm. Karen's face puce with rage as an overflowing tap flooded the yard. Cassius lying fast asleep in the shade of the big oak tree. Only when Kristy ran over to wake him, he didn't stir.

Kristy rubbed her eyes and pummelled her pillow into shape. It was only a dream, she told herself as she pulled the duvet under her chin. Cassius was safe, tucked up in his stable. She needed to sleep. She had an end-of-topic maths exam first period and she needed to do well, otherwise her parents would start nagging her about her grades again.

That's what the nightmare was all about, she realised with relief. It was a classic anxiety dream, triggered by the exam.

She had been so busy at Mill Farm she'd hardly given it a thought. But it must have been preying on her subconscious after all.

Kristy reached for the photo of Cassius on her bedside table. It was one Sofia had taken on her phone one morning when they were out hacking. Cassius was standing still, his noble head raised as he sniffed the wind. Kristy was reaching down to ruffle his mane, a big grin on her face. The hills were etched in purple behind them.

She gazed at the photo, imagining the feel of his silky mane and the delicious horsey smell of him, until her eyelids drooped. Sleep, when it finally came, was deep and dreamless.

∼

DESPITE HER FEARS, the maths test went well, and Kristy was humming cheerfully to herself as she arrived at the yard for evening stables. Everything was right with the world. Norah had decided to give them the night off, so she could fit in a short ride if she was quick. Her mum was cooking lasagne, her all-time favourite supper. Best of all, Emma had phoned to say she would be home in the morning. Kristy's days of being Karen's skivvy were almost over.

To her surprise, Karen was in the yard chatting to Viking's owner. Jean Davey was as short and round as her horse was tall and elegant. But she was quick to smile and always had a kind word for Kristy. She was also one of the owners who had offered to pitch in and help while Emma was in hospital.

Kristy headed towards the two women but as she drew close Karen turned on her heels and disappeared into the house. Kristy shook her head. The woman was so downright rude.

The back door slammed shut. Kristy realised Jean was talking.

'Sorry Jean, what were you saying?'

'It's good news about Emma. Karen was just telling me. You must be pleased everything'll soon be back to normal. I know it can't have been easy for you.'

'Working for the boss from hell? You're right, it hasn't.' Kristy knew she was probably talking out of turn but frankly she couldn't care less. Karen Miller was a tyrant. Simple as. And Kristy was used to bossy people.

'I'll help you muck them all out tonight. Goodness knows I need the exercise,' said Jean, patting her well-padded stomach.

Kristy couldn't believe her luck. 'Thanks Jean, that would be awesome. I was hoping to fit in a quick ride.'

'You do that, Kristy dear. You deserve some time off with Cassius. Although I don't know where Karen's put him. He wasn't in the bottom paddock when I rode past earlier.'

'Oh, I expect he's fast asleep under the tree.' An image of Cassius's motionless body slid, unwelcome, into her mind. She pushed it aside. It had been a nightmare, nothing more. 'Or down in the far corner. He stands so still sometimes I don't see him either.'

'I'm sure you're right. I'm as blind as a bat without my specs. Where do you want me to start?'

They worked together, Jean mucking out while Kristy filled water buckets and replaced empty haynets with the ones she'd filled the previous weekend. With Jean's help, they'd finished evening stables in just over an hour. Kristy thanked her profusely.

'It's my pleasure. Now you go and find that beautiful horse of yours and have a lovely ride. I'll see you in the morning.'

Kristy marched down the track to the bottom paddock,

Cassius's headcollar swinging from her shoulder. He'd be hiding behind the tree, or tucked in beside the hedge. Jean must have missed him. She was notoriously short-sighted without her glasses. She was always getting the twins muddled up when they were riding, even though William was about a foot taller than his sister.

But Cassius wasn't asleep under the tree. He wasn't down in the far corner, either. He wasn't even tucked in beside the hedge. Kristy criss-crossed the field, calling for her horse with a growing sense of panic. It was as though history was repeating itself. And then she skidded to a halt. He couldn't have escaped again, could he? Ended up in the house like last time?

She ran so fast back up the track her lungs were burning by the time she reached the yard. Gasping for breath, she sprinted across to the back door and wrenched it open. Not bothering to heel off her boots, she pulled the handle of the kitchen door and pushed. Nothing happened. She waggled the handle again. It must be locked. Growling with frustration she gave the door an angry kick, hopping in agony when her foot made contact with the solid oak door.

'Cassius! Are you in there?'

Silence.

Kristy dropped to her knees and pushed open the cat flap. Her ankle-high view of the room revealed table legs, chair legs and the haughty form of Bert asleep in front of the range cooker, but no horse legs.

Wherever Cassius was, it wasn't here.

10

A DEBT REPAID

*K*risty sank onto her haunches. Where could he be? Her imagination was a scramble of possibilities. Perhaps he'd been taken ill - colic? - and Karen had taken him to the vet, forgetting to tell her? Maybe he'd escaped but this time had made a beeline for the field of new wheat across the road from Mill Farm? What if she'd missed him and he was in his stable after all? Perhaps this was just another nightmare from which she would wake. She screwed her eyes closed and pinched her thigh as hard as she could. But when she opened her eyes she was still sitting on her haunches, her nose pressed against the knots in Emma's pine kitchen door.

A clickety-clack made her start and she crouched down to look through the cat flap. Two patent black stilettos were tapping their way across the stone floor tiles towards her. They stopped by the table. By swivelling her head Kristy increased the angle of her vision. Black tights, a black pencil skirt threaded with silver and a black silk shirt. Blonde hair swept back into a chignon. Karen looked smart but severe, as if she was going to a funeral. She flipped open a small silver compact and began applying lipstick with exaggerated care.

Pins and needles prickled Kristy's right foot and she shifted her weight, knocking over an empty wine bottle. She shot out a hand to catch it but missed and the bottle clattered to the floor. Risking another peek through the cat flap Kristy met Karen's eyes through the compact's tiny mirror.

'What on earth are you doing grovelling around on the floor?' she said, snapping shut the compact and dropping it into her handbag.

The last thing Kristy wanted was to give the impression she had been spying on her boss.

'I dropped a hoof pick,' she lied, reaching in her pocket for the hoof pick she always carried. 'Here it is!'

By the time she scrambled to her feet Karen had unlocked the door.

'I'm going out. Make sure you lock the tack room before you go.' She grabbed her car keys from the table and glided out of the kitchen.

'Wait! I can't find Cassius,' Kristy blurted to her retreating back.

Karen turned and regarded her steadily.

'I've looked everywhere,' said Kristy.

'Don't waste your time. He's not here.'

'What d'you mean?'

Karen looked at her watch and sighed. 'I really don't have time for this.'

'Karen, *please*. Where is he?'

The older woman tossed her bag onto the table. 'You'd better sit down.'

Kristy's legs felt cotton wool-weak and she sank into the chair, bracing herself for bad news.

'Bella Hayward came for him.'

Kristy felt winded, as though someone had punched her in the solar plexus. 'Bella *who*?'

'Arabella Hayward. Cassius's owner,' Karen said impatiently. 'She came back for him. Took him home.'

'But he's mine!'

Karen pulled open the drawer of the dresser Emma laughingly referred to as her filing cabinet. It was where she stuffed all her paperwork, from vets' bills and invoices from the feed store to the horses' passports.

'That's where you're wrong. I checked his passport. Bella's name is still on there. He's legally hers, whether you like it or not.'

'But I don't understand! She disappeared owing Emma tons of money. Emma kept him in lieu of the money she owed and my friends clubbed together to buy him from Emma for me. I've already told you this!'

'My dear sister might have taken the questionable decision to keep him, but she never updated the ownership details on his passport. And neither did you and your friends when you bought him from Emma.'

'I've never owned a horse before. I didn't know we had to!' Kristy wailed.

Karen tutted. 'It's too late now. Bella turned up last night with her rather charming fiancé, who wrote a cheque there and then. He's repaid all the money she owed. Over four thousand pounds. They sent a lorry to pick Cassius up this morning.'

Tears pricked the backs of Kristy's eyes. 'You mean he's gone?'

'Once we finally got him in the lorry. He was a devil to load. I thought at one point we might have to call out the vet to tranquillise him.'

Kristy was horrified. Cassius was the calmest, kindest horse she had ever met. 'He was probably frightened! You know he can't see properly. You need to be his eyes, tell him what's happening, so he trusts you.'

Karen gave an indifferent shrug. 'I left them to it. But brute force seemed to do the trick.'

Tears were streaming down Kristy's face. She made no attempt to wipe them away.

'Didn't you think to check with Emma?'

Karen bristled. 'I've got her four thousand pounds back. I should think she'd be pleased, wouldn't you?' She waved a hand at the tatty kitchen units and peeling paintwork. 'God knows this place could do with some money spent on it.'

A sob caught the back of Kristy's throat. Karen handed her a tissue.

'Pull yourself together for goodness sake. He's just a horse. There are plenty more where they came from. I'm sure my sister can find you a little project pony to work on.'

'I don't want a project pony. I want Cassius,' Kristy said dully. She raised bloodshot eyes to Karen. 'Where did they take him?'

'Her fiancé's place, apparently. His family owns a large estate. Lots of lovely stables, Bella said. He'll be spoilt rotten.'

'But where is it?'

'No idea.' Karen drummed her nails on the table. The sound made Kristy flinch. 'Are we done here?'

Kristy bit her lip and said nothing.

'I'll take that as a yes. Remember to lock up.' Karen gathered her bag, patted her hair and click-clacked out of the kitchen.

Kristy stared blankly after her. She felt as though her heart was being ripped in two. Her darling Cassius, her beautiful boy, had been taken from her. He could be anywhere. She might never see him again. The finality of it all brought on a fresh wave of tears.

Her worst nightmare had come true. And what made it

worse - what made it utterly unendurable - was that she had betrayed him.

She had promised to look after him, and she had broken her promise.

And she hadn't even had the chance to say goodbye.

11

CURVE BALL

*T*he journey home was a blur. Kristy stumbled along the pavement, her arms wrapped tightly around herself, wondering how her life had flipped from its regular, run-of-the-mill *ordinariness* to utter catastrophe in the space of a few seconds.

Her temples throbbed with hatred for Karen. How could she have cheerfully taken the cheque in exchange for Cassius? No piece of paper, no matter what was written on it, could ever equal his worth. Cassius was flesh and bone, heart and soul and spirit. Money was worthless in comparison. It meant nothing.

But Karen cared about money, didn't she? And so did Arabella and her stinking rich boyfriend. They thought money could fix everything, that everyone had their price. But Kristy would never have sold Cassius, not for all the money in the world.

'Are you alright?'

Kristy's heart leapfrogged into her mouth as a wrinkly hand shot out from behind a wall and rested on her arm.

'Moira, I didn't see you there!' she gasped, as the elderly

woman who lived in the apartment opposite theirs shuffled onto the pavement in front of her.

'I was just going to fetch my paper when I saw you, all hunched up as though you were carrying the weight of the world on your shoulders. Everything OK, Kristy love?'

Kristy dragged her eyes away from the pavement. Moira was looking at her anxiously, her blue eyes as faded as old denim. She straightened her shoulders and smiled bravely.

'I'm fine,' she said, fumbling in her pocket for her front door key. She jumped up the steps two at a time, aware Moira was still staring at her in concern. She let herself into their apartment and almost collided with her dad, who was carrying a coffee and the paper into the lounge.

He saw her tear-streaked face and his eyebrows shot up.

'Whatever's happened?'

Kristy may have been able to put on a brave face for Moira, but there was no way she could hide her feelings from her dad.

'It's Cassius. He's gone.'

He listened in silence as Kristy recounted her conversation with Karen.

'Surely that's illegal? Karen can't sell a horse without Emma's permission.'

'It was all perfectly legal though, don't you see? In the eyes of the law Cassius has always belonged to Arabella Hayward. He was never mine.' Kristy hiccuped softly. Her dad rubbed the salt and pepper stubble on his chin.

'I'm so sorry Kristy. I know how much you loved him.'

'Don't use past tense, Dad! I still love him, and he loves me. It's killing me that he must think I've abandoned him, after all we've been through together.'

'I'm sure he doesn't think that. As long as he's fed and watered he'll be happy. Isn't that the main thing?'

Kristy closed her eyes. An image of Cassius dozing under

the oak tree, his bottom lip drooping, filled her mind so powerfully she could almost feel the softness of his breath on her hand. 'I suppose.'

'Perhaps you'll be able to visit him once he's settled in his new home. To put your mind at rest.'

'Karen doesn't even know where he's been taken!'

'I'm sure Emma will be able to find out. She's coming out of hospital tomorrow, isn't she?'

'Think so.'

'There you are then.' Her dad patted her knee. 'Once you know where he is I'll speak to this Arabella Whateverher-nameis and explain you'd like to come and see him. You never know, she might even agree to regular visits.'

Kristy knew her dad was trying to help, but her heart still felt as if it had shattered into a million tiny pieces. 'He won't be mine though, will he, to see every day, to ride whenever I want?'

'No sweetheart, he won't. But you know something? Sometimes life throws curve balls at us. It's how we deal with them that matters. Remember when I lost my job? Our house, your school, holidays and all those lovely things we used to enjoy, like riding lessons and parties and member-ship of the golf and tennis clubs. All gone. But it hasn't stopped us, has it? Look at you, finding a job you love, making new friends and doing so well at school. Your mum still hankers after the old life, I know. But she was only saying the other day how much less time this place takes to keep clean.' He gestured at their tiny apartment. 'And me, well, I was going to save the news until dinner, but I was offered a job today. It's only as a book-keeper for the factory down the road, but it's a start.'

Kristy wiped her nose on her sleeve and braved a smile.

'That's great, Dad. I'm really pleased for you.'

'That's my girl.' He lifted her chin. 'And do you know what I'm going to spend my first month's salary on?'

Kristy shook her head.

'A new pony for you.'

'But -'

'Shush,' he smiled. 'I've made up my mind. It won't be anything flash, but it will be all yours, I promise. Now that's settled come and give your old dad a hug.'

Her dad wrapped his arms tightly round her. He smelt faintly of coffee and the lemony aftershave she'd given him for Christmas. She relaxed into his bobbly jumper. She'd always been a daddy's girl, running to him if she'd scraped her knee or fallen out with a friend. As she'd got older he was the first person she sought out when she needed advice. They viewed the world the same way, and with a few wise words he always managed to unravel even the knottiest of problems.

But this time he was wrong. She knew he meant well. He always did. And a year ago she'd have bitten off his hand if he'd offered to buy her a pony. But she didn't want any old pony. She wanted Cassius. He was her soulmate, the love of her life. They were meant to be together.

And if she couldn't have Cassius, no other pony would do.

~

KRISTY SCUTTLED past the door to the library, her head bowed. She was supposed to be meeting Sofia and the twins for a quadrille meeting, but she couldn't face their pity. Not yet.

Somehow she had made it through the morning, but her heart was heavy and the back of her throat ached with

TROPHY HORSE

unshed tears. She didn't want to talk to anyone. She needed to be on her own.

She was pushing open the double doors to the playing field when she heard her name being called. Groaning inwardly, she quickened her pace.

Norah caught up with her outside the tennis courts.

'Kristy, didn't you hear me? I was calling and calling.'

Kristy stared at the tarmac. It was slick with rain.

'I thought it was you, walking straight past the library door. William said it couldn't be, but I was right. Did you forget I'd called a meeting?'

'No.'

Norah frowned. 'So why didn't you come?'

'No point,' Kristy mumbled.

'What d'you mean, there's no point? We're supposed to be discussing costumes and who's going to make what. We've only got a couple of weeks before the centenary, remember.'

'How could I forget?' Kristy finally looked up. Something about Norah's earnest face, her perfectly-knotted tie and her navy enamel prefect badge made her snap.

'There isn't going to be a quadrille. Not with me in, anyway. Unless you want me to ride one of William's brooms,' she laughed mirthlessly.

Norah looked alarmed. 'I don't understand. Why can't you ride Cassius?'

'Because he's gone, Norah. Back to his old owner. Karen let her take him yesterday.'

Norah's eyes were wide. 'That's terrible!'

'I know.' Kristy swallowed the lump in her throat.

'But he's the star of the show. The one they all come to see.'

Anger flared deep in the pit of Kristy's stomach. 'Wait, is that all you're worried about? That you've lost your star attraction?'

67

Norah backtracked. 'Of course not! I didn't mean it like that. It's a shock, that's all. Poor you.' She went to link arms with Kristy but Kristy shook her head and pushed roughly past her.

'I don't want your pity. And you can stick your stupid quadrille, too. If Arabella Hayward hadn't seen Cassius in the paper she wouldn't have come back for him in the first place.'

As soon as she said this Kristy knew it was true. Arabella was one of those people who craved other people's trophies, like magpies coveting shiny trinkets. She hadn't wanted to know when an eye infection had stolen Cassius's sight. But his five minutes of fame had made him desirable again. Once the shine had worn off and she had become bored of him would she abandon him a second time?

And if she did, would Kristy ever be able to find him again?

12

ANNIE

Kristy trudged to the stables under pewter-grey skies that matched her mood perfectly. After leaving Norah open-mouthed outside the tennis courts, she'd stalked off to the furthest corner of the playing fields to spend the rest of the lunch-hour brooding about Cassius.

As she made her way to the humanities block for double history she'd almost collided with Miss Raven. Expecting to be reprimanded for daydreaming again, Kristy had been surprised when the head teacher had smiled benevolently.

'How's my star quadrille rider?'

A dull flush had crawled up Kristy's neck, as itchy as a rash. She cleared her throat. 'Good, thanks,' she croaked. 'Better go. I'm late for Mr Peterson.'

She should have come clean and told Miss Raven there and then her quadrille team was one short. Why hadn't she? Because a tiny part of her was still hoping it was all a bad dream and when she walked into the yard after school Cassius would be watching her over his stable door. Or that now Emma was back from hospital she would magically sort the mess out and order Arabella Hayward to bring him home where he rightfully belonged.

As it turned out, Emma had other things on her mind.

She was standing in the middle of the yard, her left arm in a sling and her right hand clutching her head in exasperation.

'That's hay, not straw! Hay is for eating, straw is for bedding. Can't you tell the difference?' she barked.

A slim girl of about nineteen with a cloud of curly hair the colour of ripened corn popped her head over the door of Viking's stable. She giggled nervously.

'Oops. I'm *always* getting them muddled up. Miss Miller says I drive her demented.'

Emma harrumphed and muttered something under her breath. It sounded like, 'I'll give her demented.'

Kristy coughed politely and Emma swung round.

'You're here. Thank goodness.' Her face softened. 'Let me introduce you to Annie and then you and I need to talk. Annie, this is Kristy, my head groom. She knows Mill Farm inside out. Check with her before you do anything, please. Understand?'

The blonde girl nodded. 'Sure. Absolutely.' Her accent was pure cut-glass.

'Kristy, this is Annie. She works at Coldblow but Karen has kindly lent her to me while I'm out of action.' Emma pulled a face and despite her black mood Kristy stifled the urge to laugh. It was clear Annie was more of a hindrance than a help.

'Annie, perhaps you could fill the water buckets? Kristy and I have a lot to catch up on.'

'Sure, absolutely, Miss Miller.'

'My sister may insist on you calling her Miss Miller but please call me Emma. We don't stand on ceremony around here.'

Annie nodded vigorously, picked up Viking's water bucket and set off for the tap at the other side of the yard.

'It's probably easier to use the hose. Saves your back,' said Kristy kindly.

Annie smacked the palm of her hand against her forehead. 'Of course! Why didn't I think of that? Clever old you.'

'No problem.'

Kristy followed Emma into the tack room, trying not to look at Cassius's empty saddle rack, and perched on the edge of the sofa.

'Hot chocolate?' Emma asked.

Kristy sprang to her feet. 'You sit down. I'll do it.'

Emma sank gratefully into the armchair. Kristy flicked the kettle on and spooned coffee into one mug and chocolate powder into the other.

'Karen told me about Cassius. I owe you an apology. I should have filled in the paperwork. I'm so sorry,' she said.

Kristy looked at Emma properly. Her face was leached of colour apart from dark bruise-like smudges under her eyes. Every time she shifted in her seat she winced in pain.

'I don't blame you,' Kristy said softly. She had spent a sleepless night directing her anger at everyone from Norah to Karen, but it wasn't fair to blame them. She sighed. 'If anything it's my fault. I should never have agreed to the interviews. I was so proud of him. I wanted to show him off. But you know what they say about pride.'

'You think Arabella saw him in the paper?'

'I'm sure of it. When he needed her most she disappeared off the face of the earth. The minute he's headline news she turns up out of the blue, wanting him back.'

Emma nodded. 'Makes sense. I had a call from her fiancé the day after the story appeared. I told him Cassius wasn't here but he insisted on coming anyway. So I hid Cassius in the kitchen and pretended to be out.'

Which explained how Cassius had managed to squeeze into the kitchen despite the locked back door, Kristy thought. 'So he didn't escape by himself after all.'

'No. I gave him a helping hand. He thought I'd gone mad. You should have seen the look he gave me.'

They shared a sad smile.

'I hoped they'd lose interest but the fiancé is obviously more lovestruck and tenacious than I gave him credit for. And absolutely rolling in money.' Emma waved his cheque in the air. 'He gave me more than Bella actually owed. I'll pay you, Sofia and the twins back your winnings, of course.'

'You can keep my share. I don't want it.'

'And I'll start paying you proper wages again, now Cassius has gone.'

Kristy shook her head. Didn't Emma get it? The money meant nothing to her. She realised her boss was talking again.

' - I know my sister has her faults, but she said she had my best interests at heart, and for once I believe her. That money couldn't have come at a better time. It means I can pay Annie while I'm out of action.'

'So Annie is one of Karen's grooms? It's nice of her to lend her to you.'

Emma grimaced. 'Nice? I'm doing Karen a favour. The girl is a complete airhead. She makes Sofia look organised. You're going to have to help me keep an eye on her.'

'She's a bit posh, isn't she? To be working in a stables, I mean.'

'She may have been born with a silver spoon in her mouth, but when it came to handing out brains she was last in the queue. She has absolutely no common sense.' Emma rolled her eyes.

'She seems nice, though.'

'You're right, she is. She's just driving me to distraction.

But she does what she's told. So I suppose I should count myself lucky to have her.'

'Do you think he'll be alright?' said Kristy suddenly.

'Cassius?'

Kristy nodded, swallowing the lump that had reappeared in her throat.

'I'm sure he'll be fine. Bella's impulsive and flaky but she was never cruel. She just blows hot and cold, that's all. One of those people who launches into a new hobby feet first and after a few months loses interest and moves onto the next thing.'

'She sounds like my cousin,' said Kristy. 'Last year it was tennis so my auntie bought her a really expensive racket and paid for hours and hours of private lessons. Now she's decided she doesn't like tennis, she wants to do triathlons. So she needs a racing bike and a wetsuit. Her mum and dad spend a fortune on all this stuff that ends up gathering dust in their garage.'

'All the gear and no idea,' agreed Emma. 'That sounds like Bella. When her parents first bought Cassius she spent every waking minute up here. She had the best tack, the nicest rugs and the most expensive riding gear. All funded by the Bank of Mum and Dad. She had weekly lessons with Karen at Coldblow, and they don't come cheap. She was obsessed. Then gradually she started coming every other day, and then a couple of times a week, and then once a week - if you were lucky. Cassius lost fitness so when she did bother to turn up and ride he wasn't the well-schooled horse she was used to.'

'Not his fault,' said Kristy.

'Absolutely not his fault,' agreed Emma. 'When his eye became infected she stopped coming at all. I heard on the grapevine she'd fallen out with her parents and they'd stopped her allowance. She's never done a day's work in her life, so of course she couldn't pay the livery fees. She's obviously found another source of income -'

' - the absolutely loaded fiancé,' supplied Kristy. 'And after seeing Cassius looking so good in the paper she decided she wanted him back. And her rich boyfriend was only too happy to oblige. It's not fair.'

Emma patted her knee. 'Unfortunately, life isn't fair. We just have to deal with it as best we can.'

'That's what Dad said,' said Kristy in a small voice.

'Then your dad is a very wise man.'

Kristy gripped her mug tightly. 'It doesn't make it any easier though, does it?'

QUADRILLE PRACTICE

K risty found evening stables strangely therapeutic. She'd assumed being at Mill Farm without Cassius would be too distressing. But the hard work involved in looking after twelve horses kept her physically and mentally busy. There was no time to wallow in self-pity. Not when there were stables to muck out, water buckets to fill and feeds to mix.

Annie was pushing a laden wheelbarrow over to the muck heap when she saw Kristy and waved. As she did the barrow hit a pothole and tipped over, emptying its entire contents in an untidy heap on the concrete.

Annie knelt down and began scrabbling the dirty straw back into the barrow with her hands. She looked around nervously. 'Where's Miss Miller?'

'In the house,' said Kristy.

Annie exhaled loudly. 'Thank goodness!'

'Why?' said Kristy, puzzled. 'Emma wouldn't mind. It's not like you did it on purpose. And you're clearing it up, aren't you?'

'Miss Miller, I mean the other Miss Miller, would have

had a meltdown. She says I'm the clumsiest, most scatter-brained, hopeless groom she has ever had the misfortune to meet. But the crosser she gets with me, the more mistakes I make, I can't seem to help it.'

Annie picked up the last of the straw and Kristy wheeled it over to the muck heap. After spending the last few days as Karen's skivvy she felt a sudden camaraderie with Annie.

'Don't worry,' she said, emptying the barrow in the furthest corner of the muck heap. 'Emma is nothing like Karen. She doesn't mind if the yard's not perfectly swept or if the forks and brooms aren't lined up in height order. As long as the horses are happy she's happy.'

Annie looked doubtful. 'She seemed rather agitated earlier.'

'I think she's still in a lot of pain from her broken arm. Come on, let's muck out the ponies together. I can show you how I do it,' said Kristy.

Annie wasn't lazy, she was just easily distracted and a bit accident-prone, Kristy decided an hour later, once they'd worked their way along the line of stables.

'What made you work at Coldblow, Annie? If you don't mind me asking?'

'Oh, well, all of my friends have tootled off to university. But that's not really my thing. I'm not the sharpest tool in the box, you see. But Daddy said it was important I do some-thing useful, so I thought, horses! And Mummy used to hunt with Karen, so she had a word and here I am. Or should I say there I was?' She giggled self-consciously. 'Oh, you know what I mean.'

'Do you hunt?' said Kristy, intrigued.

Annie shuddered. 'Absolutely not. It's like totally disgusting.'

'But it's illegal to hunt foxes in the UK any more, isn't it?'

'It is. But foxes still get caught and completely murdered,

Kristy,' she said earnestly. 'These days I am totally into animal rights. I'm even a vegetarian. Apart from bacon sandwiches, obvs.'

'Ha ha, very funny,' chuckled Kristy.

Annie's eyes widened. 'I wasn't joking. I absolutely *adore* bacon. It's to *die* for. I could never give it up.'

'Right,' said Kristy. Annie really was something else. But she couldn't help warming to her. 'We'd better get the horses in.'

Kristy handed Annie Viking's headcollar and hoped she wasn't as hopeless at handling horses as she was at stable management. But she needn't have worried. Annie walked up to the big bay gelding, talking all the time. She ran a hand along his neck and whispered something in his ear. Kristy watched in amazement as Viking dropped his head low so she could fix his headcollar and then followed her meekly out of the field.

'He seems to like you,' said Kristy. 'He can be tricky with new people.'

'All horses are like this with me. I seem to have a bit of a gift for it. Daddy calls me the Horse Whisperer,' said Annie.

Kristy studied her face for signs of conceit or jocularity, but her expression was serious and utterly without guile.

'I think that's why Miss Miller puts up with me,' Annie admitted.

One by one they brought the horses in. The minute Annie had blown softly into their noses, scratched them behind their ears or rubbed their withers they were all putty in her hands, even Norah's pony Silver, who had a tendency to nip if he thought he could get away with it.

'Who lives there?' asked Annie, as they walked past Cassius's empty stable.

'No-one,' said Kristy shortly.

'Hey, did I say something wrong?'

Kristy silently remonstrated with herself. It wasn't Annie's fault Cassius had gone. She made herself smile. 'Of course you didn't,' she said.

She checked her watch. It was almost six. Sofia and the twins would be arriving soon, ready for their quadrille practice. She still wasn't sure she could face them. She handed Annie a broom and ducked into the feed room.

'Can you sweep the yard while I mix the feeds?'

'Sure, absolutely,' said Annie.

'And if anyone asks, I'm not here.'

Annie looked puzzled. 'So who's going to mix the feeds?'

'I am,' said Kristy patiently. 'Just pretend you haven't seen me.'

'But you're standing right in front of me.' Annie's face cleared and she slapped a palm against her forehead. 'Oh, I get it. You don't want someone to know you're here.'

Kristy nodded as a car door clunked shut. 'And there they are. So I've gone home, OK?'

Annie gave a mock salute and giggled. 'Message received and understood.'

Kristy squeezed behind the feed room door, ducking to avoid a dusty cobweb. She listened as Annie introduced herself to Sofia and the twins.

'Where's Kristy?' Norah barked.

'Oh, um, she's definitely not in the feed room,' said Annie.

Kristy raised her eyes. Annie really was hopeless.

'Actually I think she might have gone home. Is there anything I can help you with?'

'Have you wet Silver's hay?' Norah asked imperiously. 'He's allergic to dust. I'm sure Kristy must have mentioned it.'

Kristy remembered the day she met Norah for the first time. She had been just as bossy. Still was in fact.

Their voices faded as they crossed the yard, probably to check if Silver's hay had been properly soaked. Kristy edged out from behind the door and eased open the lid of the feed bin. If she started mixing the horses' feeds now she could take them out while Sofia and the twins were in the school practising their routine.

She was just scooping chaff into Jigsaw's bucket when Sofia marched in.

'You *are* here!' she said. 'I thought Annie looked a bit shifty. Are you trying to avoid us?'

Kristy flushed. 'Sorry.'

'You are silly. We're your *friends*, Kristy. We're on your side. Ever since Norah told me what happened I've been so worried about you. I'm so, so sorry.' Sofia looked close to tears. Kristy felt her own eyes smart.

She shrugged. 'Everyone's sorry. But being sorry isn't going to bring him back.'

'There must be something we can do? We bought him for you, after all. Surely if we told this woman how upset you are, how Cassius needs you, she'd understand.'

'That kind of thing only happens in stories, Sof. Not in real life. In real life people don't give a monkey's about anyone else. They're just out for themselves,' Kristy said bitterly.

A flash of alarm crossed Sofia's face. 'But we could at least try -'

'Don't bother. Anyway, I need to get on. And you've got quadrille practice, haven't you? I'm sure Norah's stressed enough about having to re-do the routine for three people without you being late for practice.'

'What d'you mean three people?'

'She didn't tell you everything then. I'm not doing it. How can I? I don't have a horse any more, remember.'

'That's where you're wrong,' said an indistinct voice behind them. Kristy spun around in surprise.

'Emma, I thought you were having a rest!'

Emma stepped out of the shadows. She was holding a notebook in her good hand and a pencil between her teeth.

'You know me, I can't sit still,' she mumbled around the pencil. 'I thought I'd do a stock take of feed.'

'What do you mean, Kristy's wrong?' said Sofia.

Emma took the pencil out. 'She does have a horse.'

Hope flared in Kristy's heart. Perhaps Emma had tracked Arabella down and bought Cassius back. Perhaps he was even now in the back of a horse lorry, wending his way home to her. The urge to fling her arms around his neck and bury her face in his thick mane was so overwhelming that for a minute she forgot to breathe.

'She can ride Jigsaw.'

'Perfect!' said Sofia.

'Jigsaw?' said Kristy. The tiny flicker of hope died, like fire in a vacuum. 'I don't want to ride Jigsaw. I want to ride Cassius, and if I can't ride Cassius then I'm not riding anyone. Now if you'll please leave me alone, I have horses to feed.' She picked up two buckets and pushed past Sofia to the door.

PRETTY PLEASE

*S*trains of music followed Kristy around the yard like a particularly annoying younger sibling as she fed the last of the horses and scrubbed buckets for the following day.

Inside the brightly-lit indoor school she could hear Norah barking orders at Sofia and William over the sound of the music. Phrases like 'Change the rein!' 'Wrong leg!' 'I said canter circles not oblongs!' were carried out on the evening breeze.

Kristy was transported back to the previous autumn, when they'd spent hours together practising their routine for the New Year's Eve show. Norah had driven her mad, and they'd had to work so hard, but it had been a blast.

Kristy wasn't in any hurry to get home and she found herself being drawn to the bright lights of the indoor school. Just five minutes, she told herself, slipping in through the open door.

Annie was sitting on an upturned bucket in the corner, her eyes shining. Kristy joined her.

'This looks such fun!' said Annie in a stage whisper.

Norah glared at Kristy as if she was the one who was talking.

Kristy held a finger to her lips. Annie nodded and they watched the rest of the routine in silence.

The longer Kristy watched, the more uncomfortable she felt. Guilt prickled as painfully as nettle rash. It was all too obvious. Norah's beautifully symmetrical routine worked perfectly for four horses. It probably worked for two, and maybe even for six, but for three it looked awkward and unbalanced. Norah obviously thought so, too, as she was getting redder and redder in the face, and her voice more and more ragged as she shouted instructions to William and Sofia.

As they rode up the centre line three abreast Norah didn't bother to salute. She slithered off Silver and dragged him over to Kristy and Annie.

Kristy had never seen her looking so disheartened. Usually she was so assured.

'I don't know why we're bothering, I really don't. It's hopeless with three people!'

'It's not that bad,' lied Kristy.

'No, you're right. It's so much worse. Miss Raven's expecting perfection! This is a shambles!'

'I thought you were all super,' said Annie.

Norah ignored her and smiled imploringly at Kristy. 'Sofia told us Emma offered to lend you Jigsaw.'

'And I told her I wouldn't be taking her up on her offer anytime soon.'

Norah clasped her hands together as if she was praying. 'Please Kristy, we need you.'

'Why can't people take no for an answer?' Kristy grumbled. Secretly she was enjoying watching Norah grovel. It made a welcome change. And a tiny part of her felt flattered they needed her so much.

'Pretty please?' said Norah.

Kristy imagined riding Jigsaw into the ring at the centenary. He was a showy horse, bigger than Cassius and with beautiful floaty paces. He was a real head turner. Everyone would be impressed.

Why was she refusing to take Emma up on this amazing offer? Loyalty to Cassius, or plain stubbornness? Kristy knew in her heart Cassius wouldn't mind. He loved her unconditionally. Her mum would say she was cutting off her nose to spite her face. And she was right. In a second Kristy realised she had been an idiot. She smiled at Norah.

'I'll do it! I'll ride Jigsaw,' said Annie suddenly.

The smile on Kristy's face froze. Norah's hands fell to her sides.

'Really?'

'I'd love to. It looks so much fun!'

Norah looked her up and down. 'You can ride, I assume?'

Annie looked worried. 'I've competed at intermediate level dressage. Would that be good enough?'

Norah grinned. 'You bet it would!'

'But Annie doesn't go to our school,' said Kristy.

'Miss Raven won't mind. Not when I tell her we were let down by our fourth team member.' Norah shot Kristy a filthy look. She looked over her shoulder at Sofia and William, who had jumped off their ponies and were wandering over.

'I've found a replacement for Kristy,' she crowed.

'You'd better check Emma doesn't mind Annie riding her horse,' said Kristy.

Norah narrowed her eyes. 'When did you last compete at intermediate level dressage, Kristy Moore? Never, that's when. Of course she won't mind. Come on, Annie. We'll go and ask her now.'

As Norah dragged Silver behind her Kristy could have sworn the little grey gelding gave her a look of sympathy.

Sofia and William were staring helplessly at Norah's retreating figure.

'You two make a right pair, if only you could see it. You're both as stubborn as each other,' William said crossly.

'We'd much rather you were on the team. Annie seems nice enough. But it won't be the same without you,' said Sofia.

'I know,' Kristy finally admitted. 'I've been an idiot,' she said glumly. 'But it's too late now, isn't it?'

～

ANY MISGIVINGS EMMA may have had about the change of jockey were swept aside by Norah's legendary powers of persuasion. By the time Emma found Kristy in the hay barn, listlessly filling haynets, it was a done deal.

'I hope you're not upset, but you did say you didn't want to ride him, didn't you?' she said.

'I know. And it's fine. Honestly.'

'When people say 'honestly it's fine' it usually isn't,' said Emma shrewdly.

Kristy shrugged. 'It serves me right for being pig-headed. Call it an important life lesson. I really will be fine.' She pulled the haynet tight and tossed it into the corner of the barn. 'At least I would be, if I could only see Cassius one last time.'

Emma raised her eyebrows.

Kristy took a deep breath. The idea must have been floating around her subconscious for a while, and as she started talking it became blindingly obvious. 'I want to see where he's living. So I can picture him there, you know?'

Emma said nothing but Kristy was on a roll. 'I want to check he's OK, for my own peace of mind. I want to explain to Arabella what he's been through. How he needs her to step up and be his eyes. I want to make sure she's totally committed this time, and isn't going to lose interest and take up snowboarding instead. Most of all, I want to say goodbye. Properly. Tell him I'll always be there for him. That I'll always love him.' Kristy's voice wobbled and she took a deep breath. 'So that's what I'm going to do.'

~

SOFIA SAT at their favourite table in the library, her head bent over a book. Kristy hitched her rucksack further up her shoulder and zigzagged past desks and chairs to reach her. She sat down with a thump.

'So what's she like?'

Sofia placed her bookmark in her book and lay it carefully on the desk in front of her.

'You really want to know?'

'Yes. No. Oh, I don't know. Just put me out of my misery and tell me.'

'She rides like a dream. Jigsaw goes beautifully for her. Emma watched our training session last night. I could have sworn she had a tear in her eye.'

'I'm so pleased,' said Kristy, her voice heavy with sarcasm.

'You did ask,' said Sofia mildly. 'Norah's cock-a-hoop.'

'I bet she is.' Kristy played with the strap of her bag. 'Sof, I've got a massive favour to ask.'

'I don't think Norah's going to change her mind now, Kristy. Sorry.'

'No, it's not that. I want to find out where Cassius has gone. Just to check he's OK. But I don't really know where to start. Will you help?'

'Of course I will!' Sofia held up her index finger. 'On one condition.'

'Name it.'

'You help us get ready for the quadrille.'

Kristy's eyebrows shot up. 'What, become the team skivvy so Norah can spend every waking hour bossing me about? No thanks!'

'No, not skivvy. I was thinking you could help in more of a coaching capacity. Come along to training sessions and tell us where we're going wrong.'

Kristy gave a bark of laughter. 'Oh yes, because Norah's going to love that.'

Sofia shrugged. 'Leave her to me.'

'But why do you want me tagging along? You've got Annie now.'

'Come on Kristy, it won't be the same if you're not involved in the team.'

Kristy curled her feet around the legs of her chair. Being stubborn hadn't done her any favours last time. 'And if I do agree, and it's a big if, will you help me find Cassius?'

Sofia smiled broadly. '*When* you agree, of course I will!'

NEW COACH

K risty waited a beat.
'Alright, I'll do it.'

Sofia gave a little fist pump. She reached in her bag for her rough book, unscrewed the lid of her fountain pen, jotted something down and underlined it twice. Kristy swivelled her head to read it. *Finding Cassius*, it said.

'I've always fancied becoming a private detective. You can be my first client. So, Miss Moore, tell me what you know.'

Kristy thought back to her conversation with Karen. 'Arabella's fiancé bought Cassius back for her. He's loaded. Drives a red sports car. He seems to be bank-rolling her.'

'A sugar daddy?'

'No. He's not very old. Early twenties at most, I should think. He told Karen his family owned a large estate with lots of stables and that's where they were taking Cassius. Only she didn't think to get the address.'

'And what is his name?'

Kristy shrugged helplessly. 'I have no idea.'

'Our first dead end.' Sofia chewed a strand of her long red hair. 'Let's try a different tack. What's Arabella's last name?'

'Hayward.'

'Mmm, quite a common name.' Sofia reached into her bag for her phone. 'I'll try Googling her. We need to find out where she lives.'

'That's easy, Emma will know. She was a livery, remember. We'll ask her tonight.'

~

FOR THE FIRST time since Cassius had gone Kristy felt optimistic. She had a plan. Sofia was helping her. And, although she wouldn't be admitting as much to Norah, a tiny bit of her was glad to be involved with the team. She was even looking forward to tonight's training session. Sofia had promised to clear Kristy's new role with Norah before the end of school.

As she sat through double maths Kristy's mind wandered from the trigonometry she was supposed to be studying to their search for Arabella Hayward. Perhaps, if she played her cards right, Arabella would be happy for her to visit Cassius occasionally. She might let Kristy have the odd hack out when she was too busy to ride. Some of the liveries at Mill Farm had sharers who rode once or twice a week in return for a contribution towards the livery fees. OK, so money didn't seem to be an issue, but perhaps Kristy could offer to poo pick or muck out in return for a ride.

By the time she reached the yard she had everything worked out. She and Arabella would hit it off instantly, and Arabella would be grateful for Kristy's offer of help. She must be frantically planning her wedding, Kristy reasoned. While she was busy being Bridezilla, choosing menus and venues and whatever else a bride-to-be needed to do, Kristy could be exercising Cassius. It was the perfect solution.

Expecting to find the yard as reassuringly scruffy as it usually was, Kristy did a double take. The place was immaculate. The concrete was perfectly swept and the stables were all mucked out. Someone had even coaxed the muck-heap into some kind of order. Hearing Annie humming to herself in the tack room, Kristy wandered over.

'Hi Kristy! Everything's done. They just need bringing in,' Annie said.

'You're kidding.'

'I came over early. As a thank-you for Miss Miller letting me ride Jigsaw.'

'Cool.' Kristy slung Henry's headcollar over her shoulder. 'I'm going to be helping out a bit. With the team,' she added.

Annie's face lit up. 'Awesome! I'm so totally excited about it. It's going to be so much fun!'

Kristy smiled back. 'It will. And don't mind Norah. She can be a bit bossy but she means well. Most of the time, anyway.'

By the time Kristy and Annie had brought the horses in the twins and Sofia had arrived. Kristy finished fixing the straps on Viking's rug and crossed the yard to where Norah was picking out Silver's feet.

She lay a hand on the little gelding's withers and took a deep breath. 'About Sofia's idea,' she began.

Norah let go of Silver's hoof and eyed Kristy coldly. 'What about it?'

'I just wanted to check you were cool with it and everything.'

'What, the fact you refused to join the team but you're more than happy to order us all around?'

Kristy gripped Silver's mane. 'It wasn't like that!' she squeaked defensively.

Norah's lip curled. 'Oh yeah?'

'Absolutely! Sofia promised to help me find Cassius but only on the condition I helped with the quadrille. She didn't really give me a choice.'

'Ah, I see. You're only offering to help because you have to, not because you want to?'

Kristy shot a desperate look towards Jazz's stable, but Sofia was nowhere to be seen. 'What do you want me to say, Norah? That I do want to help or I don't? Help me out here.'

Turning away, Norah picked up Silver's back foot. To Kristy's alarm her shoulders were shaking with fury. She mentally kicked herself for agreeing to Sofia's demands. She should have known how Norah would react. She was a control freak, and control freaks never like relinquishing their control to anyone.

She hovered for a few moments more, until she became aware of a snorting noise. Norah seemed to be struggling for breath.

Kristy leant down, her hand on Norah's shoulder. 'Are you OK?'

Norah's face was screwed up and a tear was rolling down her cheek. But she wasn't cross or crying.

'Hey, why are you laughing?'

Norah set Silver's foot on the ground and howled with glee. 'You should have seen your face! And the way you tip-toed across the yard. It was priceless! Honestly Kristy, you're so easy to wind up.'

Realisation dawned. 'You mean you were kidding me?'

Norah wiped the tear from her cheek. 'I couldn't resist. You looked so *earnest*. People think William's the only one with a sense of humour. But I can out-prank the best of them.' She chuckled to herself.

'So you don't mind me helping out?'

'No, I don't mind, Kristy,' Norah said patiently. 'I can't ride *and* keep my eye on everyone. Emma hasn't got time to help. You know our strengths and weaknesses and you know the routine. It'll be good to have you on board.'

Kristy exhaled slowly. 'Thank you. I'm glad that's sorted.'

Norah handed the muddy hoof pick to Kristy and smiled sweetly, but there was a steel-like glint in her eye. 'But don't go getting any ideas above your station. You may have been brought in as a temporary advisor, but I'm still the boss, alright?'

SUPER SLEUTHS

*K*risty stood in the middle of the school, her hands in her pockets. One by one the others walked past her. Annie first, riding with a long rein so Jigsaw could stretch his neck. Sofia was right. Annie was a great rider, balanced and perfectly in tune with the big skewbald gelding. William next on Copper, who was totally unfazed by the fact his rider was sitting back to front in the saddle and was making faces at his sister behind them. Pointedly ignoring her twin, Norah was wittering on about their training schedule for the next few days. Bringing up the rear was Sofia on Jazz. The highly-strung mare was tossing her pale golden head and crabbing up the side of the indoor school, still brimming with energy even though she'd worked her four white socks off for the last hour.

It had been a good session. Kristy always tried hardest for the nicest teachers at school, so she had decided to use the same principle in her new role as temporary advisor. Encouraging and generous with her compliments when they did well, she refused to fix on their faults. It seemed to have worked. Norah had positively burst with pride when Kristy had praised her perfect ten metre circles. And as they turned into the centre of the school the four riders looked flushed and happy.

'Well done, that was awesome,' said Kristy.

'And you're a natural teacher. Counting the canter beat out loud really helped me keep Jazz's rhythm steady. Where did you learn that?' said Sofia.

'In one of my pony magazines, I think. I used to do it when I was schooling Cassius.'

Sofia patted Jazz and jumped off. 'Now it's time for me to keep my end of the bargain.'

They found Emma in the kitchen, washing up one-handed.

Sofia marched over to the sink. 'I'll do that. Kristy's got something to tell you.'

Emma wiped her hand on her jeans. 'Go on, spit it out. What catastrophe has she caused now?'

'Annie?' said Kristy, surprised. 'She hasn't caused any catastrophe. In fact she's worked really hard today. And she seems to have really clicked with Jigsaw.'

Emma nodded grudgingly. 'I have to admit she does have a way with horses, even if she is a liability around the yard. So what did you want to tell me?'

Kristy chose her words carefully. 'You know I said I wanted to find Cassius?'

Emma frowned. 'I'm sorry Kristy, I'm not sure it's a good idea.'

'Why?'

'What are you going to gain from it? It'll only upset you.'

Kristy had decided not to share her plan to win Arabella Hayward over and inveigle her way back into Cassius's life. She didn't want anyone pouring scorn on her dreams. She placed her hand on her heart. 'I won't get upset, I promise. I just want to see him one last time.'

'So what do you want from me?'

'Bella's address. You must still have it from when she was a livery.'

Emma looked conflicted. 'I do. But -'

'*Please* Emma.'

Emma sighed. 'Alright then. But don't say I didn't warn you. And don't tell the Haywards how you came by their address. I don't want any comeback. Client confidentiality and all that.'

She reached into the drawer of the dresser, pulled out a black leather address book, licked her thumb and flicked through it. 'There it is. The Old Coach House, South Street. You know where it is?'

Sofia peeled off her rubber gloves. 'It's that private road at the back of the hospital, isn't it? Very posh.'

'That's the one. I have a phone number, too, if you want it?'

Kristy shook her head. 'It's way too complicated to explain over the phone. Sofia's going to come with me, aren't you Sof?'

Sofia nodded and linked arms with her. 'Don't worry, Emma. I'll look after her.'

～

THE TWO GIRLS stood outside The Old Coach House and gazed up at its impressive brick facade.

'Wow,' said Kristy, her stomach a knot of nerves.

'How the other half live.' Sofia's voice was wry. 'Shall we see if the Haywards are home?'

Kristy flashed Sofia a smile. 'No time like the present.'

They crunched up the gravel drive, passing a formal knot garden and lichen-covered statues of Greek gods and goddesses. A sleek metallic grey Mercedes was parked outside the front door.

'At least someone's at home,' Sofia whispered.

Kristy took a deep breath and rapped on the door. After a beat it swung open to reveal a tiny grey-haired woman wearing a paisley housecoat and an enquiring smile.

Kristy stepped forward. 'Mrs Hayward?'

The woman erupted in peals of laughter. 'I'm Shirley, the housekeeper. Mrs Hayward's at her bridge club. Can I help you, love?'

'We were wondering if Arabella was home?' said Kristy.

Shirley glanced furtively behind her. 'Bella?'

'Yes,' said Kristy patiently. 'Is she home?'

The housekeeper beckoned them closer. 'Bella doesn't live here any more. She and her father had a falling out. They'd been clashing more and more. And after that business with the horse -'

'What business?' said Kristy sharply.

'Mr Hayward said he'd finally had enough of her capricious ways. Said he was disinheriting her. He didn't mean it, of course. She's always been the apple of his eye. But she stormed off and we haven't seen hide nor hair of her since. Her parents are devastated.'

'So you don't know where she is?' said Kristy with a sinking heart.

Shirley shook her head sadly. 'And now we're not allowed to talk about her. It's as if they can't bear to hear her name.'

'Shirley, is someone at the door?' said a gruff voice from deep inside the house.

The housekeeper flinched.

'Only some girls wondering if we've any odd jobs need doing, Mr Hayward.'

They stiffened at the sound of footsteps on flagstones. Shirley glanced behind her again. 'You need to go!' she hissed. She started pushing the door closed. But Kristy was too quick, jamming it open with her foot.

'You must know something that might help us find her, Shirley. Please, try to think. It's really important,' she implored.

The housekeeper shook her head. 'I told you, we've no idea where she's gone. All I know is when I was cleaning her room after she'd left I found a note on her dressing table.'

'What did it say?' said Sofia impatiently.

'Call me Teddy. And a mobile number.'

'Have you still got it?'

Shirley shook her head. 'I didn't think to keep it. I threw it in the recycling.'

The sound of footsteps grew louder. Shirley held a finger to her lips and the two girls nodded. Kristy took a step back just as the door creaked open. A tall, slightly stooped man whose forehead was puckered with frown lines looked them up and down.

Kristy smiled brightly. 'We were just telling your house-keeper we're looking for odd jobs. Gardening, car washing, that kind of thing.'

'Very enterprising I'm sure,' said Mr Hayward. 'But I can't help you, I'm afraid. Good day.'

And Kristy and Sofia watched helplessly as the door clicked shut in front of them.

～

'WHY WOULD Bella want people to call her Teddy?' Sofia whispered, as they tramped back down the drive. 'Do you think she wanted to change her identity so her parents couldn't find her? If so, why choose a boy's name? It doesn't make sense.'

Kristy shook her head impatiently. 'I don't think the note said 'call me Teddy'. I reckon it said 'call me. Full stop. Teddy'.

Sofia's brow crinkled and then her face cleared. 'Oh I *see*. It was a note from someone called Teddy asking Bella to call him. Like, for a first date or something?'

Kristy nodded. 'What if Bella did call Teddy, and they got on so well they had a whirlwind romance? What if Teddy is the man I saw at Mill Farm, the man looking for Cassius?' She turned to Sofia with shining eyes. 'What if Teddy is the mysterious rich fiancé?'

'It's a lead, that's for sure. But it doesn't really get us anywhere. We have no idea who Teddy is or where we might find him.'

Kristy's shoulders slumped. 'Another dead end.'

'Not necessarily. Teddy's quite an unusual name. There can't be too many of them around here who drive a red sports car and live on a big estate.'

'If only Shirley had kept that note,' Kristy wailed.

'Life is full of if onlys, Kristy. The fact is she didn't. We just need to find another way to track him down.'

17

TOO MUCH FIZZ

*K*risty lay in bed, wide-eyed and restless. Something had been bugging her ever since she and Sofia had gone their separate ways at the end of the Hayward's long drive. Something she'd missed. An important clue that could lead her to Teddy.

She tossed and turned under her duvet. Sleep was impossible. Her mind was in overdrive as she replayed Teddy's visit to the yard and every conversation she'd had about him with Emma and Karen. She picked it all apart, word by word, to see what nugget of information about Bella's mysterious fiancé she might have missed. But whatever it was, it stayed tantalisingly out of reach.

She yawned and checked her clock. It was half past midnight. If she didn't get to sleep soon she'd be in no fit state for their practice session the next day. She put Teddy firmly to the back of her mind and ran through the quadrille routine in her head over and over until she finally grew drowsy.

Then, in the brief moment between wakefulness and sleep, she had a second of lucidity. Her eyes snapped open and she sat bolt upright. What an idiot she'd been! Teddy had written Emma a cheque to cover Bella's debts, hadn't he? Hardly anyone used cheques any more when bank transfers were so much faster. But Teddy was obviously the old-fashioned type. And he would have signed the cheque. All she had to do was ask Emma to show it to her and she would have his last name.

Kristy felt a spark of hope that she might finally be a step closer to finding Cassius and she smiled into the darkness. 'Not long now, Cass, I know it,' she whispered. 'Just stay safe until I find you.'

~

KRISTY JOGGED down the Mill Farm drive, desperate to speak to Emma. School had dragged so slowly she had at times wondered if someone had somehow pushed the pause button on her life forcing time to stand still.

At last, after a tortuous biology lesson in which Kristy had fidgeted so much her teacher had asked if she needed to use the lavatory, the final bell sounded. Kristy exhaled so loudly the boy sitting at the desk in front of her looked around in astonishment. She had jumped to her feet, scooped up her books and darted out of the classroom before the bell had finished ringing.

Pelting towards her locker as fast as a human tornado, Kristy silently congratulated herself on her forward planning. Tucked under her PE kit was a carrier bag containing her jodhpur boots, jods, a spare top and a cereal bar. It meant she could go straight from school to the stables, saving at least half an hour.

But when she arrived at Mill Farm there was no sign of Emma's Land Rover or Annie. The yard was empty save for

Marmalade, who was spreadeagled in a patch of sunlight on the dusty concrete.

'Where's Emma, Marmalade?' Kristy asked, hoping her boss hadn't decided to drive one handed to the feed store. But the cat just stared at her, his pupils wide and his eyes unblinking. Kristy tickled his chin and headed for the barn. There was no-one there. The tack room and feed room were also empty.

'Where can they be?' Kristy muttered to herself.

At that moment the silence was broken by the asthmatic belch of a diesel engine. Kristy spun around. Emma's Land Rover was leapfrogging down the track, narrowly missing the gatepost as it lurched into the yard and ground to a halt a couple of metres in front of her.

'Look where you're going, for goodness sake!' shrieked a familiar voice from the passenger seat. 'That's my head groom you nearly knocked over!'

The driver's door opened and Annie hopped out, a sheepish look on her face. 'She's a bit tense,' she mouthed to Kristy, dipping her head in Emma's direction. 'I think I might make myself scarce. Give her time to calm down a bit. Honestly, she gets more like her sister every day. Though thinking about it, my driving instructors were all the same.'

'How many did you have?' said Kristy, bemused.

'Four. They were all as jumpy as Emma. I can't think why. I'll see you later for practice, OK?'

Kristy suppressed a smile and went around to the passenger side.

'Everything alright, boss?' she said, opening the door and bracing herself for a verbal onslaught.

'No, it is not alright! The dozy girl offered to take me to hospital for my check-up. She claimed she could drive. Well, she's about as good at driving as I am at flame throwing. Which, surprise surprise, is not very good at all. Honestly, my blood pressure is through the roof. Forget painkillers, it's tranquillisers I need!'

'You're here now,' said Kristy in a placatory voice. She unclipped Emma's seatbelt and held out her arm. 'How about I make you a nice cup of tea?'

Once Emma was settled at the kitchen table with a mug in front of her, Kristy felt able to broach the question she'd been dying to ask all day.

'You know the cheque Bella's fiancé wrote to cover the livery fees and stuff? Do you still have it?'

'Why d'you ask?'

'I was thinking it would have his details on. To help, you know, track him down.'

Emma sighed. 'You're not still fixated about finding Cassius are you? I hoped you'd get over that.'

Kristy bit her lip. As if she could ever get over him. 'Do you still have the cheque?' she repeated.

Her heart sank as Emma shook her head. 'I cashed it this afternoon. The gormless girl dropped me off at the bank before my hospital appointment. Nearly took out a man on a mobility scooter while she was parking, mind you.'

'So you haven't got it?' said Kristy in a small voice.

'Afraid not.' Seeing the dejection on Kristy's face, her expression softened. 'I'm sorry.'

'It's OK. It was worth a try. You weren't to know. I'd better go and help Annie bring the horses in.'

Kristy was pulling on her wellies outside the back door when Emma called out, 'I can remember his name if that's any help?'

She dropped the boot she was holding and dashed back into the kitchen.

'You can?'

Emma nodded. 'It was an unusual name. Teddy. I

remember wondering who on earth would call their son after a teddy bear.'

Kristy nodded to herself. Her theory about the note was right. Teddy and Bella must have hit it off. 'Teddy what?' she asked expectantly.

'Oh, it was something really commonplace.' Emma's face clouded over. 'I'm really sorry, Kristy. I can't remember.'

~

KRISTY KNEW she mustn't let her disappointment spoil the quadrille practice so she pasted on a smile and beckoned the team over.

'OK, so we know we can't practice the whole routine too many times otherwise the ponies and Jigsaw will get stale. They'll start anticipating the moves before you've given them your aids, and it will all go horribly wrong.'

The twins, Sofia and Annie nodded.

'So we're going to work through different elements indi-vidually until they are perfect, like the serpentines and circles and crossovers. Then we'll have a couple of run-throughs of the whole thing before the actual day.'

'Which is only a week on Saturday,' said Norah.

'Ten days' time,' agreed Kristy. 'So today we're going to practice the windscreen wiper. I think it's probably the trick-iest manoeuvre in the whole routine, don't you?'

William nodded vigorously. 'It's really hard to keep Copper in line with Silver. He's so slow.'

'He's not slow!' cried Norah indignantly. 'He can't help having shorter legs!'

Kristy held up her hands. The last thing she needed was to referee a fight between the twins. 'It's a good discipline to be able to extend and collect your trot, so that's what we'll work on today.'

Once they had warmed up with a few trot and canter circles Kristy called them over again. 'So if you remember, you've just ridden a serpentine down the school. When you all reach A you ride your windscreen wiper back up.'

'I can't remember where I'm supposed to be,' said Sofia.

Kristy gave her a smile. 'I know, it's hard to remember out of context, isn't it? Norah's on the inside, then you, then William, with Annie and Jigsaw on the outside.'

Norah clicked her tongue and Silver bustled into position. The others lined up beside her.

'What I really want to practice today is synchronisation and accuracy,' said Kristy. 'I want you all to keep a steady tempo and be totally aware of everyone else so you can temper your pace to match the others. We want to be turning at exactly the same time and keeping even spacing, so when we reach E and C we're still perfectly in line, just like you are now.'

Jazz chose that moment to spook at a swallow in the eaves of the school and shot forward like a racehorse out of the starting gate.

Norah tutted. 'Not like that!'

'Sorry,' mouthed Sofia, collecting her mare and riding back in line.

'No worries. So let's give it a go, shall we?' Kristy jogged to the far end of the school. 'Go large to get a nice working trot going and start the windscreen wiper at A.'

Riding four abreast, they trotted around the school. With Silver and Norah on the inside and Annie and Jigsaw on the outside it should have been relatively easy to stay in line, but Jazz was so full of beans Sofia was struggling to keep her in check and as they drew level with A she was already half a length in front of the others.

'Steady Jazz,' Sofia muttered. The mare flicked a golden ear back and spun sideways into Copper. Fortunately the chestnut gelding, who was as laid-back as William, took no notice. But Jigsaw had picked up on Jazz's excitement and began cantering on the spot.

As they completed their wavy windscreen wiper only Silver and Copper stayed in line. Kristy sighed inwardly. All four lined up in front of her and looked at her expectantly.

She fished around for something positive to say. 'This certainly gives us something to work on,' she said eventually. 'Shall we run through it again?'

After several more attempts Jigsaw at least had calmed down but Jazz was still skittering about like a lamb with a bellyful of spring grass. Kristy checked her watch. It was half past six.

'Let's call it a night. And I'm giving you tomorrow off. I think a long hack might be in order for Jazz, to try and get rid of all her energy.'

Sofia held her reins lightly as the mare jogged around the school. 'I don't know what's got into her. I suppose it's not that new stuff I bought her?'

'What new stuff?' said Kristy.

'It's a conditioning and performance supplement. Hadn't you noticed how shiny her coat is at the moment?'

Kristy looked Jazz up and down. Her palomino coat was certainly silky smooth with a beautiful sheen. The bits that weren't dark with sweat, anyway.

'Jazz is fizzy enough as it is, Sof. I really don't think she needs a performance supplement. We need her calm and sensible for the quadrille, not so over-excited and full of energy she won't listen to you. Can you perhaps leave off the supplement until after the quadrille?'

'I suppose,' said Sofia, looking longingly at her pony's glossy quarters.

'Give some to Silver instead,' smirked William. 'Either that or a rocket up his -'

'William!' scolded Kristy in her best schoolteacher's voice. 'That's enough!'

'I hate you!' shrieked Norah to her brother, swinging Silver around and trotting out of the school in high umbrage.

Kristy stared at the ceiling and counted to ten. Deep down she had known she'd need the patience of a saint to corral these four into some semblance of order. But honestly, they were driving her mad!

'Don't forget, patience is a virtue, Kristy Moore,' she intoned to herself as she followed the others out of the school. 'Patience is a virtue.'

18

GOODBYE CASSIUS

risty flipped the laptop closed and picked up her notebook, studying it with narrowed eyes. She had spent the last hour flipping between Google Maps and Street View trying to pinpoint all the large country estates and farms within a ten mile radius of Mill Farm Stables. There were forty three. And that didn't include smallholdings. Cycling to each of them to see if they belonged to the mysterious Teddy would take a month of Sundays.

She sighed. Detectives on the TV were dangled handy clues at regular intervals so they at least stood a chance of finding their man. But real life was proving much less accommodating. How was she supposed to find Cassius when the only clues she had were a first name, a cherry-red sports car and an anonymous country estate?

Think outside the box, she told herself. Could the sports car lead her to Teddy? But she couldn't even remember what make it was, let alone the registration plate. And even if she did, she could hardly go to the police and ask them to look it up on their computer. Teddy may have broken her heart by buying Cassius back for Arabella, but he hadn't committed a crime.

No, it was useless. She might as well resign herself to the fact she was never going to see Cassius again. Ever. She tossed the notebook on her bed and reached for the photo on her bedside table. She traced a finger along Cassius's familiar face, lingering over his narrow blaze shaped like a bolt of lightning. Memories of the first time she'd ever seen him came flooding back. She'd been leading Silver down to the bottom paddock on her very first day at Mill Farm when she'd spied him watching her from the far corner of the field. Kristy couldn't speak for Cassius, but for her it had been love at first sight. Something about his proud yet gentle nature had melted her heart and she'd fallen for him hook, line and sinker.

When Emma had asked Kristy to ride Cassius she had been over the moon, but at the back of her mind she'd always known they were on borrowed time. Emma had never tried to hide the fact she needed to sell the Percheron. But then Sofia and the twins had bought him for her and Kristy had been given her fairytale ending.

Only she hadn't, had she? The fairytale ending had been a mirage. Her Happy Ever After nothing more than an illusion. It turned out her dreams had been built on shifting sand. The moment Arabella had decided she wanted her trophy horse back, fate had stepped in and dealt its cruel blow.

And Kristy's fairytale ending had shattered as easily as glass.

❧

THAT NIGHT KRISTY's dreams were once again filled with Cassius. In the first he was standing at the top of a mountain, calling for her. In a panic, Kristy climbed up to meet him. But the further she scrambled up the rocky scree the further away he seemed. She pushed herself harder and harder until her lungs felt as if they were going to explode, but when she looked up he was as small as a pinprick, a tiny black dot on the horizon.

'CASSIUS!' she yelled, but her voice was carried away by the wind, as insubstantial as a dandelion seed.

Suddenly she was in the tack room at Mill Farm watching Sofia and the twins lounging on the moth-eaten old sofa. Sitting on one of the armchairs with her back to Kristy was a girl with a stair-rod straight back and long blonde hair. She was holding court while the other three listened with rapt expressions.

'Annie is no longer riding in the quadrille. I will be taking her place,' the blonde girl announced.

'Cool,' said Norah ingratiatingly. 'Are you riding Jigsaw, Bella?'

The girl gave a tinkly laugh as cold as crystal. 'Of course I won't, idiot child. I will be riding my beautiful Cassius.'

He's not yours, Kristy tried to say. But the walls of the tack room dissolved and all at once she was standing under the oak tree in the bottom paddock, Cassius asleep in front of her.

'Cass,' she called softly. He must have heard as his eyes snapped open and he said in a deep voice as rich as melted chocolate, 'I've been waiting for you, Kristy. I knew you'd come in the end.'

'Oh Cassius, I've missed you so much,' she cried, flinging her arms around his neck and snuggling close. 'I'm so sorry I never had the chance to say goodbye.'

'There's nothing to be sorry for. You found me, didn't you?'

'But only in my dreams,' Kristy sobbed.

Cassius curled his neck around her and she felt the warmth of his breath on her skin.

'Don't be sad, Kristy,' he said. 'You'll always be able to find me in your dreams.'

When Kristy woke the next morning her duvet was a tangled mess and her arms were wrapped around her pillow. To her surprise she felt clear-headed and strangely content. Cassius knew she loved him, and nothing could ever take that away. And one day she would find him.

Until then she had a quadrille team to lick into shape.

≈

'THOSE TEN METRE circles have been bothering me,' said Kristy as Sofia, the twins and Annie lined up in front of her at their next practice session.

'Why? You said mine were "perfect",' said Norah, wiggling her index fingers in the air.

'And they are. You are an example to us all. But Copper has a tendency to fall in halfway around, Jazz needs to bend her body, not just her neck, and Jigsaw has always finished his before the rest of you are three quarters of the way around yours, which ruins the symmetry. Another danger is when you hit the edge of the school. The ponies start following the track out of habit and suddenly you're riding in a straight line.'

'And there are no straight lines in circles,' said Annie.

'There definitely aren't,' Kristy agreed.

'I always find it hard to judge how big ten metres is,' said Sofia.

'Me too,' admitted Kristy. 'It helps me to remember the school is twenty metres wide, so - and I know it sounds obvious - ten metre circles are half the width of the school.

So if you're circling at B or E you need to be hitting X every time.'

'OK clever clogs, how do I stop Copper falling in?' said William.

'I've been reading up on that,' said Kristy. 'When you feel as though he's becoming unbalanced and doing his motor-bike lean you need to open your outside rein and use your inside leg. Why don't you try it with a ten metre circle at B?'

They watched as William and Copper picked up a trot.

'Look up and where you're going. Ask for flexion just before B and remember, outside rein, inside leg,' Kristy called.

Copper's ears were pricked as he left the track at B. William clicked his tongue and the chestnut gelding swished his tail. Kristy could see he was beginning to fall in but William opened his outside rein and used his inside leg on the girth to push him back into a circle. Once they were back on the track they went large and William eased Copper into a walk.

'Good job!' said Kristy. She turned to Sofia. 'I think your inside leg is the key to getting Jazz to bend, too.'

'I'll give it a go,' said Sofia. Jazz had been marginally calmer since Sofia had stopped giving her the conditioning supplement, but she still arched her neck and crabbed onto the track when Sofia asked her for a trot.

'Give her a good canter to use up some of her energy. We need her to listen to you,' said Kristy. Once Jazz had cantered around the school a couple of times on each rein Sofia brought her back to a working trot. Following William's lead, she used her inside leg and outside rein as she rode her ten metre circle, her face a picture of concentration as she asked her mare not just for flexion but for her to bend her whole body.

'Much better,' said Kristy. 'And now for you, Annie. I

know you and Jigsaw can do a beautiful collected trot - I've seen you do it. But you need to be watching the others to make sure Jigsaw doesn't out-pace them. Why don't you and Norah ride up the centre line and trot a ten metre circle at X, seeing if you can keep together?'

'This is harder than it looks,' puffed Annie, as she struggled to collect the big skewbald gelding. Jigsaw finished his circle a length and a half ahead of Silver.

'You don't want to lose momentum, you just want him to keep a compact outline and take shorter, higher steps. And remember to watch Norah so you can judge your pace,' said Kristy.

After half a dozen more circles Jigsaw and Silver were almost matching each other stride for stride. Kristy decided to quit while they were ahead and gathered her team for a final pep talk.

'That was brilliant. The twenty metre circles will be a cinch now. We'll put that into practice again tomorrow, this time with the music, and we'll have one run-through of the whole routine before our dress rehearsal next Thursday.'

'Don't you think we should squeeze in a couple more practice sessions? I want it to be perfect, not just good enough,' Norah fretted.

'Absolutely not. I don't want the ponies getting stale,' said Kristy firmly.

'Are you sure you haven't been sneaking lessons at the Norah Bergman School of Bossiness?' quipped William as they filed out of the school.

'You have become very assertive recently,' agreed Sofia. 'Not that I'm complaining,' she added hastily. 'I know we all need keeping in line.'

Kristy giggled. Her heart felt lighter than it had for ages.

'You think that's bossy? Haha, you ain't seen nothing yet!'

19

DRESS REHEARSAL

The days slipped by in a whirlwind of preparations. There were manes to pull and tails to trim. Tack to clean and plaits to practice. The thrum of anticipation at Mill Farm reminded Kristy of the busy days before the New Year's Eve show, as they'd put their finishing touches to a performance that, despite the odds, had clinched them first place.

She realised she wasn't the only one reminiscing when they sat in the tack room with their usual hot chocolates after their last practice session before the dress rehearsal. It had gone well, apart from an awkward moment when an over-enthusiastic Jigsaw had almost collided with Copper as they'd threaded the needle.

'At least none of the horses have gone lame this time,' said William, blowing on his hot chocolate.

'Don't tempt fate!' Norah screeched. 'Quick, touch wood everyone.'

They all touched the wooden crate that doubled up as a coffee table.

'And I haven't left my costume on the bus. Not yet, anyway,' giggled Sofia.

'Kristy had to teach me to vault last time, do you remember?' said Norah.

Kristy nodded. 'And then I went and vaulted straight over Cassius and landed on the wrong side. I felt like a proper charlie.'

'It didn't matter though, did it?' said Sofia.

'They loved us,' Norah agreed.

They gazed at their silver cup, which had pride of place on the shelf above the sink.

'And then you all did the nicest thing anyone has ever done for me,' Kristy said quietly. 'I'll never forget that, you know.'

Sofia patted Kristy's arm. 'Cassius was our lucky charm.'

Kristy gave a sad smile. 'My luck ran out in the end though, didn't it?'

~

AT SCHOOL, signs of the centenary celebration started appearing. Extra chairs were stacked high in the hall, ready to be carried onto the playing field by the strongest sixth-formers. The school band could be heard practising in the music room every lunchtime. Teachers, preoccupied with the preparations, were too busy to set homework, to the delight of their classes. The gym was out of bounds as the gymnastics club practised their routine over and over, their music playing on a loop.

'I hope they don't get stale,' joked William as he and Kristy walked past on their way to the library one lunchtime.

Finally the day of the dress rehearsal arrived. Kristy and Emma settled down to watch.

'I've got butterflies,' Kristy admitted. 'I'm as nervous as if I was riding myself!'

Emma patted her arm. 'It's only natural. You've invested as much as they have in this routine. Of course you want them to do well. How do the costumes look?'

'I don't know. They haven't let me see them yet. They wanted it to be a surprise.'

'You've enjoyed helping them, haven't you? It seems to have taken your mind off Cassius.'

Kristy nodded. She knew the yearning she felt for the big Percheron would never go away, but over the last few days it had lessened from a stabbing agony to a dull ache.

'Close your eyes, Kristy!' shouted Norah.

Kristy did as she was told. She heard muffled hoof prints and the clink of bits as her friends rode in.

'OK, you can open them now.'

Kristy opened her eyes and gasped. The ponies and Jigsaw were immaculately turned out, their coats gleaming. The girls, in their checked pinafores and straw boaters atop their riding hats, looked as if they had stepped out of the pages of a history book. William had the impish grin and raggedy clothes of a street urchin. Norah and Sofia had made the horses matching blankets and bandages out of hessian sacks. With one dappled grey, a palomino, a chestnut and a skewbald, Silver, Jazz, Copper and Jigsaw were never going to match, but the hessian rugs and bandages pulled the look together, and made them look like a team.

'You look amazing!' breathed Kristy.

'Very impressive,' agreed Emma.

'Pretend you're Miss Raven,' said Norah. She glanced at the others. 'Ready?' They nodded. 'Cue music!' she called and Kristy flicked the CD player on.

On the count of three they trotted up the centre line and saluted as one.

'They've been practising their salute,' Kristy muttered. 'Perhaps they have been listening to me after all.'

'I'd say so,' said Emma approvingly. 'They're doing great.'

She was right. As they circled and criss-crossed the school, the three ponies and Jigsaw were calm, collected and completely in tune. Kristy noticed how Sofia, Annie and the twins continuously flicked looks at each other to gauge their tempo so they could match their pace. They turned at the same time and were exactly opposite each other in the mirrored elements like the ten metre circles and the canter circles. The threading the needle was slick and their windscreen wiper faultless. Kristy was mesmerised.

As they halted for the final salute Kristy and Emma jumped to their feet to give them a standing ovation.

'Awesome job!' Kristy cried, patting the ponies one by one. She felt an inexplicable urge to cry. *Happy tears*, she told herself.

And they were. She couldn't have been prouder if she'd ridden the quadrille herself. They'd done a great job between them.

Norah slithered to the ground, handed her reins to Kristy and stepped onto one of the upturned buckets.

'As team leader I'd like to say a few words. Kristy, obviously we would all rather you were riding Cassius in the quadrille. No offence, Annie.'

Annie smiled. 'None taken.'

'But as that wasn't possible, we are just really, really pleased you agreed to help. I know you weren't sure about it to begin with, but we want you to know we couldn't have done this without you. So thank you, from the bottom of our hearts.'

Kristy swallowed the lump in her throat. 'My pleasure,' she croaked.

'So are we ready?' shouted William.

Kristy beamed at them all. They were her friends. Her *team*. They needed her as much as she needed them. And she was so proud of them. She high-fived Norah.

'Are you ready? You bet you are!'

20

JIGSAW'S FLIGHT

*a*n orange sun as plump as a satsuma was peeping over the horizon as Kristy peered out of her bedroom window on the morning of the centenary. She'd set her alarm extra early, determined to show Norah she could be as organised as she was. But if Kristy thought she would be the first to arrive, she was wrong. As she pushed her bike into the yard Annie was already there, giving Jigsaw a bath. The older girl saw Kristy and grimaced.

'His white bits are yellow, no matter how many times I wash them. And his tail is a disaster!'

Kristy gave her a reassuring smile. 'Norah's got some special blue shampoo for greys. I'm sure she won't mind you having a bit. I'll see if I can find it.' She disappeared into the tack room. The shampoo was poking out of Norah's grooming box.

'There you go. Norah swears by it.'

'Thanks,' said Annie, fanning herself. 'Hot isn't it?'

'Not especially.' Although it promised to be a beautiful day the air was still crisp and Kristy was glad of her fleece.

She looked at Annie properly for the first time. 'Are you OK? You look like you've seen a ghost.'

'I didn't get much sleep. One minute I was shivering, the next I was boiling hot. I expect it's nerves.'

'Maybe,' said Kristy doubtfully. Annie had dark shadows under her eyes and her skin had a greyish tinge to it. 'Are you sure you're not ill?'

'Don't be daft. I'll be fine. But I might get a drink, if that's OK? Can you keep an eye on Jigsaw?'

'I'll do better than that,' said Kristy, rolling up her sleeves. 'I'll finish washing him.' She tweaked the gelding's ear and he gave her a friendly nudge. Soon she was elbow-deep in the bucket of soapy water, working the shampoo into suds. She dipped Emma's rubber mitt in and worked the suds into his coat in a circular motion, concentrating on his white patches.

One she was happy with his body she dipped his tail in the bucket and used her fingers to work in a generous squirt of shampoo. It was immensely satisfying, watching the water turn grimier and his tail cleaner, even if it still wasn't quite as white as Annie's complexion. Next she turned her attention to his mane. By the time Annie reappeared, her hands wrapped around a mug of coffee, Kristy was rinsing him off with the hose.

'You drink your coffee. I'll dry him off.' Kristy rummaged around in the grooming box for a scraper.

'You're an angel,' said Annie.

Was it Kristy's imagination or did Annie's voice sound shaky?

'Did you used to get nervous before dressage competitions?' she asked.

Annie shook her head. 'That's the weird thing. I never did. Perhaps it's the thought of performing in front of a load of teachers. I was always so useless at school.' She laughed, but it turned into a cough. 'Oh look, the twins are here.'

The next couple of hours flew by as they washed the three ponies, plaited manes and oiled hooves. Kristy checked her watch. It was a quarter to ten.

'You'd better get changed. We need to be gone in fifteen minutes.'

'Alright, bossy boots,' said Norah.

Kristy smiled sweetly. 'I learnt from a master.'

Norah tutted, but her eyes were twinkling. 'Haha, very funny, I'm sure.'

Once they reappeared in their costumes Kristy lined them up beside their horses so she could take a photo. She smiled.

'You look amazing. Miss Raven is going to be super impressed.' She consulted her clipboard. 'Ponies, tick. Riders,' she glanced briefly at Annie, who was staring vacantly into space but was at least present and correct. 'Tick. Music?'

'I gave it to the school secretary on Friday,' said Norah.

'Excellent,' said Kristy, ticking it off her list.

'Everyone ready?'

'Tick!' Sofia and the twins chorused.

Kristy grinned.

'Nutters,' she said fondly. She realised it didn't matter she wasn't riding. She was just glad to be part of it all. She felt a stab of sadness Jigsaw was there in Cassius's place. But she was determined find him, no matter how long it took. Her priority today was to help her friends perform an unforgettable quadrille worthy of their school's one hundredth birthday.

She checked Jigsaw's girth. Annie was gripping the reins so tightly her knuckles bulged.

'Are you *sure* you're OK?' Kristy whispered.

'I do feel a bit…spacey. But I'll be fine.'

'Is Emma coming to watch?' asked Sofia, trying to soothe an over-excited Jazz.

'My mum and dad are picking her up at half past,' said Kristy. 'Right, are we all set?'

The others nodded.

'Then let's do this!'

Kristy pedalled in front of the others, stopping every now and then so they could catch her up. It was only a couple of miles to their school if they went the back way. They should be there by half ten, which gave them plenty of time for last minute preparations before their performance at eleven.

As they rounded the corner to the school Kristy's eyes widened. Length after length of bunting in the school colours of navy and plum adorned the metal railings and navy and plum helium balloons tied to the gateposts danced crazily in the breeze. Every space in the car park had been taken up and people had doubled parked in the road outside.

'Crikey, there are loads of people here,' said Norah, who always suffered from last minute nerves.

'Not as many as there were at the New Year's Eve show,' said William reassuringly. 'And anyway, we'll be fine. We've practised so hard for this.'

Norah flashed her brother a quick smile. 'You're right.'

'Miss Raven said we're to go in through the side gate,' Kristy reminded them, holding her breath as Jazz shied at the balloons, her eyes on stalks.

'Steady girl,' said Sofia, hardly moving in the saddle.

'William, you go first. Copper's bombproof,' instructed Kristy. 'Jazz next, then Silver and Jigsaw.'

Sofia followed William past the balloons without incident. Silver spooked but Norah was ready for him. She gave him a pony club kick in the ribs and he crabbed past with flared nostrils. But when Jigsaw clocked the balloons he span around in panic and clattered down the lane, sparks flying from his hooves. Annie shrieked and Kristy clutched her handlebars and stared after them in horror.

'William, go after them!' cried Norah.

'No,' said Kristy, thinking quickly. 'Jigsaw might think it's a race and go faster. If I cut across the school fields I can intercept them at the end of the road. It's got to be worth a try.'

Kristy hauled her bike around and set off, pedalling furiously down the school drive, past the humanities block and tennis courts and across the playing fields, where the school band was already playing to hundreds of people. She skirted around the back of the crowds, bouncing over tussocks and dodging errant toddlers.

There was an area in the far corner where the wire fence sagged and sixth-formers sneaked out at lunchtime to head into town. Kristy powered towards it, her shoulders hunched over the handlebars and her thighs burning.

At last she reached the corner and flung her bike down in the grass. In the distance she could hear the pounding of hooves. She listened carefully. There were three beats. Jigsaw must have slowed to a canter at least. She sprinted to the junction where the lane met the main road. Cars tore down the road, oblivious to the ton of horse bearing down on them.

Shielding the sun from her eyes, Kristy waited for Jigsaw to appear around the bend in the road. When he did her heart skipped a beat. He was riderless. Annie must have fallen off.

Kristy ran beside the main road, waving her arms frantically. A showroom-shiny saloon car slowed, and she waved her hands even more furiously.

'Stop!' she cried, and the saloon slowed to a halt beside her. The window whirred open and the driver, an elderly man in a trilby hat, beckoned her closer with long, bony fingers. Kristy leant in. The plush interior had the unmistakable whiff of brand new car about it.

'Has there been an accident?' he said.

'Not yet, but there will be,' said Kristy breathlessly. 'There's a bolting horse and he's coming this way. I need to stop him before he gets to the main road.'

'Shall I call the police?'

Kristy shook her head. 'No time.' She glanced desperately behind her. She could see Jigsaw in the distance. He was growing bigger with every stride. Suddenly she had a brain-wave. 'Can you park your car across the road? That should stop him.'

The old man raised bushy eyebrows. 'And if it doesn't?'

'It will,' said Kristy. 'So can you do it? *Please?*'

The man nodded once, turned the ignition and the engine purred into life. He glanced in his rear-view mirror and manoeuvred the car so it was parked across the road.

It was just in time. Jigsaw was now so close Kristy could see the whites of his eyes. His stirrups flapped against the saddle, increasing his panic. Kristy walked slowly forward, her eyes fixed on the gelding's face and her arms outstretched.

'Whoa,' she called. Even to her own ears she sounded high-pitched and panicky. She took two deep breaths and tried to steady her voice.

'Steady, Jigsaw, there's a good lad. It's alright. There's nothing to be frightened of.'

The gelding's pace faltered and Kristy took another couple of steps forward. 'Whoa,' she crooned. Jigsaw's ears flicked forward.

He's listening to me, she thought jubilantly.

Cymbals crashed shrilly as the school band reached a crescendo. Jigsaw quickened his pace to a four-beat gallop.

For one terrifying moment Kristy thought the big gelding was going to leap over both her and the car. But she stepped forward and spoke to him again, as calmly as she could. He hesitated and Kristy reached up to grab his reins.

Her hands closed over the leather and Jigsaw skidded to a halt with all four legs braced, wrenching the muscles in her shoulder. He was no more than a metre from the car. Kristy's legs almost buckled beneath her as she realised how narrowly they had avoided disaster.

Jigsaw was blowing heavily, his flanks heaving like a pair of bellows. Kristy tightened her grip on his reins and stroked his neck, talking to him softly.

The old man climbed stiffly out of his car and joined her.

'That was brave,' he said.

'Or stupid,' she admitted. 'Thank you so much. Your lovely new car, it could have been completely trashed.'

'Ah, it's only a car,' he said, doffing his trilby at her. 'At my age you realise what's really important. And you two, will you be alright?'

Kristy swallowed. Her shoulder stabbed with pain, she had no idea where Annie was and the quadrille was due to start in about fifteen minutes. But Jigsaw was safe. That was the most important thing.

She leant against the big gelding and nodded. 'We will.'

21

MANE ATTRACTION

*K*risty ran up Jigsaw's stirrups and loosened his girth a couple of notches. She felt his legs for signs of heat, relieved he appeared remarkably unscathed. Once she was sure he'd stopped blowing she turned him back up the road towards the school. Her bike could wait. The big gelding walked beside her docilely.

Half expecting to find Annie lying in the middle of the road clutching a broken bone, Kristy was surprised it was empty apart from the odd straggler, late for the centenary celebration. She tightened her grip on the reins as she led Jigsaw past the balloons, but he didn't even flinch.

'You old fraud,' she told him.

She spied Silver's dappled rump beside the tennis courts and quickened her pace. It was five to eleven. As long as Annie was OK they could still make it - just.

William was the first to see them. He waved frantically and shouted something to the others, who spun around and watched them approach with open mouths.

Kristy's eyes searched for Annie. Her parents and Emma were there, and William, Sofia and Norah were all on their ponies. But there was no sign of Annie. Kristy's blood ran cold as she pictured her on a stretcher being carried into the back of an ambulance.

Norah and Silver were heading straight for them.

'Oh thank goodness you're here,' she said.

'Where's Annie?'

Norah waved a dismissive hand. 'In the back of your car. She's fine. She didn't even fall off. She managed to pull Jigsaw up, got off because she said she felt dizzy, and then he took fright again and she let go of his reins, the silly idiot.'

'Norah, she can hear you!' cried Sofia, pointing to the open car window.

'I don't care,' said Norah. 'She's let us down big time.'

Kristy's mind was working overtime. 'You'll be OK. You've done it with three before. Just remember when you ride up the centre line to spread yourselves out a bit more and -'

'We're not doing it with three,' said Norah.

'I know it's not ideal, but needs must. There are only three of you,' Kristy pointed out.

'Ah, but that's where you're wrong. There are four of us.'

It took a moment for Norah's words to sink in. Kristy shook her head. 'Don't be silly. I can't do it. I've never ridden Jigsaw before, I don't know the routine and I can't wear this,' she said, looking down at her faded jeans and sweatshirt.

'Number one, you'll be fine riding Jigsaw. You're just as good a rider as Annie.' Norah shot a filthy look in the direction of the open car window. 'Number two, you probably know the routine better than all of us. You've watched us doing it enough times. And number three, Annie's already changed into some of your old clothes your mum found in the boot. So you can wear her outfit.'

'But -'

'*Please*, Kristy. Do it for the team?'

Kristy looked imploringly at her parents and Emma, who had joined the three children.

'Come on, kiddo, you can do it,' said her dad.

Emma nodded. 'Jigsaw'll look after you. He rides like a dream.'

'Unless he sees a balloon,' said Kristy, playing for time. If she procrastinated for long enough they'd have to go on without her.

'There aren't any balloons on the playing field, I've checked,' said her mum.

'What would Cassius say?' said William. 'If he wasn't a horse,' he added.

Blushing as she remembered how Cassius had spoken to her in her dream, Kristy pictured his kind, wise face and her heart ached. He had loved performing in front of everyone at the New Year's Eve show. Of course he would want her to go out there and strut her stuff. 'Alright, I'll do it,' she muttered.

Sofia whooped and William punched the air. Norah jumped off Silver, rummaged around on the passenger seat of the car and handed Kristy the spare costume. 'You've got precisely three minutes. Go!'

Kristy's stomach was somersaulting. She wasn't sure if it was with nerves or excitement. She dived into the back of the car to change. Annie was sitting in the passenger seat, wrapped in their tartan picnic blanket. Her teeth were chattering.

'Are you OK?' said Kristy.

'Your mum reckons I've got the flu. She's going to drop me home after the show. I'll be fine after a couple of days in bed.'

'You don't mind if I take your place, do you?' Kristy asked.

''Course I don't. You'll love Jigsaw. Just remember one vital thing,' said Annie.

'What?' said Kristy.

'He hates balloons.'

~

EMMA WAS HOLDING Jigsaw with her good hand. His head was high and his nostrils quivering as he watched the proceedings. He suddenly seemed enormous and Kristy was gripped by panic.

'I don't think I can do it,' she croaked.

Emma was brusque. 'Of course you can. He's a push button ride.'

'But I don't know which buttons to push!' Kristy cried.

'Take five deep breaths and calm yourself down. You don't want to transmit your nerves to him, do you?'

Kristy shook her head.

'Good. So listen to me, Kristy Moore. You are the best stable hand I have ever had. You have a lovely way with horses. Just look at Jigsaw now.'

The big gelding had dropped his head and was nuzzling the pockets of Kristy's pinafore dress, hoping for a treat.

'Jigsaw knows you and he trusts you. And he will try his heart out for you. So don't be a wimp and get on and ride!'

Kristy checked his girth and pulled down his stirrups. Her dad gave her a leg up and she stroked Jigsaw's neck.

'Ready?' called Norah.

Kristy looked down and met Emma's eye.

'Have a bit of faith in yourself,' her boss said softly. 'You can do it.'

Kristy dipped her head. Emma was right, she could.

She gathered her reins and grinned at them all. 'Ready!'

~

HALF A DOZEN SIXTH-FORMERS were clearing away the mini

trampolines and wooden horses the gymnasts had used in their routine. The quadrille was the penultimate performance, and was to be followed by a parade of children wearing the school's many uniforms and sports kits over the years.

The four riders lined up at the far end of the hockey pitch, Norah with Sofia, Kristy beside William. Adrenalin flowed through Kristy's veins, kicking her nerves into touch. She felt alert and completely focussed on the task ahead.

Beneath her, Jigsaw shifted his weight as they waited for Miss Raven's cue to go. The skewbald gelding was bigger than Cassius by half a hand and was much narrower than her beloved Percheron. She was glad they'd ditched the vaulting.

The loudspeaker crackled and Miss Raven's voice carried across the playing field towards them.

'Thank you to our talented gymnasts for a truly excellent performance. And now it is my great pleasure to introduce our very own quadrille team, Mane Attraction!'

'Mane Attraction?' spluttered William. 'Sis, what were you thinking?'

Norah was puzzled. 'It's a play on words. A pun.'

'It's cheesy, that's what it is.'

'Neigh, it's not,' said Sofia.

'Yeah, why the long face? Don't be a neigh-sayer, William,' said Kristy, giggling.

She was still grinning like an idiot as they trotted into the ring and stopped in front of their headmistress. Holding their reins in their left hands, they dropped their right hands to their sides and nodded as one. Miss Raven acknowledged their salute with an approving smile and a dip of her head. The first uplifting notes of their music filled the air and they were off.

Norah and William peeled off to the right and Kristy followed Sofia to the left. Jigsaw's stride was longer than

Cassius's but when she asked him to collect he did so immediately, shortening his stride so she could keep half a length's distance between him and Jazz. Their crossover at X was as accurate as any they'd done in their practice sessions and when they passed Norah and William at the bottom of the arena the twins were grinning as widely as Kristy was.

They followed Jazz's golden rump up the long side of the arena and crossed the diagonal again at X.

'Canter circles,' Norah muttered out of the corner of her mouth as they passed each other again. But she needn't have worried. Kristy had watched the others practice the routine so many times she could picture every move with perfect clarity. A few strides before she sat deeply in the saddle and as they passed C she squeezed her inside rein, moved her outside leg slightly behind Jigsaw's girth and nudged his side. She breathed a sigh of relief as he struck off on the correct leg. The faces of the spectators were a blur as they cantered a full circle. Jigsaw's canter was so balanced and he felt so light in her hand that although she had to trot across the diagonal Kristy knew he would have executed a perfect flying change if she had only asked him to. So it was with a stab of reluctance she half-halted him and asked for a trot at H so she could change reins.

But soon she was cantering again, exhilarating in the feeling of the powerful horse beneath her. The crowds were clapping along to the music now, but Jigsaw took it all in his long, balanced stride. Emma was right, Kristy thought. He really was a push-button horse.

At X they slowed to a trot and changed rein. As they paired up again at A William raised his eyebrows at Kristy.

'Alright?' he mouthed.

'Never better,' she grinned.

Norah and Sofia turned off the centre line for their ten metre circles. William and Kristy followed suit. When they rejoined the centre line they lined up behind Norah and rode a serpentine down the school and their wavy windscreen wiper back up again. It took all of Kristy's concentration to keep the long-strided skewbald gelding in line with the others, especially as they all had to keep pace with Silver. Norah's face was stiff with concentration as she teased an extended trot out of her stout little pony.

'Nearly there,' Kristy murmured to Jigsaw. The gelding flicked an ear back at the sound of her voice. She realised she didn't want the quadrille to end. But the music was building to a crescendo and they just had one final arc of the school to complete before they rode back up the centre line and took the final salute.

Children and adults alike cheered as they stopped in front of Miss Raven once more, flushed and triumphant. Kristy felt as light as air. All the petty squabbles, the power struggles, the tears and the tantrums were forgotten. Once again they had smashed it. Four best friends doing what they did best.

'Beautifully done. You are all a credit to the school,' said the head teacher, stepping forward to stroke each of the horses' noses in turn. When she reached Jigsaw she paused and looked up at Kristy. 'Norah told me what happened to your horse and I am very sorry. If there's anything I can do to help -'

Kristy shook her head. 'There's nothing anyone can do. But thank you anyway.'

22

TEDDY

*T*he other three were re-living their five minutes of fame but Kristy suddenly had no appetite for it.

'What's up, sweetheart?' said her dad.

'I hope you're not sickening for something, too,' said her mum, feeling her forehead.

'I'm fine, Mum. Don't fuss,' said Kristy, brushing her hand away. And then to the others, 'Can we go now?'

She jumped back in the saddle before they could reply and rode towards the side gate. From her sixteen hands high vantage point she had an eagle-eye view and she watched as the crowds streamed towards the main entrance of the school.

She let the reins slip through her hands so Jigsaw could stretch his neck. He had looked after her today, no question. Not many horses would perform so well for a strange rider.

She caught a glimpse of a man in her peripheral vision. Something about his bearing snagged a memory. It was the way he walked - with a swagger, as if he thought the world was watching him. Kristy twisted in her saddle to get a better look. He was talking animatedly to a girl with long

135

blonde hair. She had her back to Kristy. But his face was in profile as he whispered in her ear and she doubled up with laughter.

It was Bella Hayward's boyfriend Teddy. And if that was Teddy, the girl with long blonde hair must be Bella. And Bella knew where Cassius was. Kristy had to talk to her. It might be her only chance.

She gathered her reins and pushed Jigsaw into a trot. The big gelding responded immediately, scattering families in all directions as they tried to avoid his pounding hooves.

'Bella!' yelled Kristy at the top of her voice. 'Bella Hayward!' Everyone within earshot spun around to see what the commotion was about. Everyone, that is, except Bella and Teddy, who were so engrossed in conversation they can't have heard her.

They'd reached the main gate and everyone slowed to squeeze through. Realising Jigsaw was about to be hemmed in by dozens of people Kristy had no choice but to ease him back into a walk and then stop him altogether. She craned her neck and watched helplessly as Bella and Teddy drifted out of the gate and disappeared.

'Come *on*!' muttered Kristy to the crowds. But they refused to go any faster. Suddenly she had a brainwave. If she headed down to the far end of the playing field to the science labs there was a gap in the fence for the school's ride-on mower. If she could reach it in time she could double back through the staff car park and catch up with them at the front of the school. It had to be worth a try.

Norah watched, open-mouthed, as Kristy swung Jigsaw round and headed in the opposite direction.

'Where are you going?' she cried, but Kristy cupped her hand behind her ear and shook her head, as if she couldn't hear her.

Jigsaw, glad to be free of the crowds, broke into an easy

canter the second Kristy asked and soon they were careering down to the far corner of the field.

If Miss Raven saw them now she was as good as dead, Kristy thought, glancing behind her and wincing when she saw the hoof marks Jigsaw was cutting into the playing fields so lovingly tended by the school caretaker, Mr Arnold.

They had almost reached the gap when she heard the sound of thundering hooves behind her. Easing Jigsaw back to a walk she looked back to see Sofia and Jazz bearing down on them.

'What's wrong, Kristy?'

'I saw Bella. She's here!' she cried.

Sofia looked puzzled. There was no-one within a hundred metres of them. 'Where?'

'That's the point,' said Kristy impatiently. 'They disappeared through the main entrance. I'm going to try to cut them off before they leave.'

'I'll come with you. Strength in numbers and all that. What does she look like?'

'Long blonde hair. She's with a tall fair-headed guy. That's her fiancé, Teddy. I've never met her but I recognised him from when he came to Mill Farm looking for Cass.'

They clip-clopped behind the science labs, heading for the tennis courts.

'Uh oh,' said Sofia.

'What is it?'

Sofia nodded towards the sports hall. 'Mr Arnold.'

Kristy swallowed. If the caretaker realised they had trashed his playing fields they'd be for the high jump. Metaphorically-speaking, of course.

'You know the film Madagascar?' Sofia hissed.

'What's that got to do with anything,' Kristy whispered back.

'Be a penguin.'

'A *penguin?*'

'Smile and wave, Kristy. Smile and wave.'

They did exactly that, pasting broad grins on their faces and waving enthusiastically at the caretaker. Caught off-guard, he waved and smiled back.

'Works every time,' said Sofia with satisfaction. 'See her yet?'

Kristy had been scanning the crowds of people looking for two blond heads but with no luck.

'It's no good. We've missed them,' she said flatly.

'Wait, that's not them is it?' Sofia said, pointing to a couple in the middle of the throng of people.

Kristy squinted into the sun. 'The woman's about forty and the man's grey, not blond,' she said.

Jigsaw stopped. Kristy clicked her tongue and squeezed her legs but he didn't budge.

'I think he needs a wee,' said Sofia.

'All over the tennis courts! You've got to be kidding me, Jigsaw. Mr Arnold will go ballistic,' groaned Kristy. She stood up in her stirrups, trying to look as nonchalant as possible as half a dozen people turned their heads to see what was causing the sound of gushing water. Remembering Sofia's mantra, she smiled and waved at a couple. And then her eyes locked onto two blond heads bobbing towards the parked cars.

'There they are,' Kristy shrieked, sitting back down in the saddle and giving Jigsaw a kick. But the big skewbald was going nowhere until he was ready. And that, judging by the sound of it, wasn't anytime soon. She looked at Sofia in desperation.

'I'll go,' Sofia said and Kristy could only watch as Jazz crabbed sideways along the court towards the car park.

By the time Jigsaw had given a satisfied grunt and started walking, Sofia and Jazz had long disappeared. So had most of the people. Only the last few stragglers remained. Kristy pushed Jigsaw into a trot and found Sofia waiting for her beside the main school gates. She was alone.

One look at her face told Kristy everything she needed to know.

'I'm so sorry, Kristy. We were too late. They were just getting into their car and by the time I'd caught up with them they'd raced off.'

'It's not your fault,' said Kristy dully.

'It was a red sports car. I've memorised the numberplate if it helps?'

'Not really. But thanks for trying. It's another dead end. I have no way of tracking them down.'

'Oh but you do!' said Sofia, her green eyes sparkling.

'What do you mean?'

'They were here, weren't they?'

'Yes, but -'

'And Miss Raven said it was invite only...'

A lightbulb in Kristy's head glowed yellow and she grinned. Of course, it was obvious. 'So Miss Raven must have sent them their invite. She must know where they live.'

23

FORTUNE FAVOURS THE BRAVE

*M*iss Raven operated a traffic light system outside her office. If the light above her door gleamed red, fellow teachers and students alike knew disturbing her would have dire consequences. Amber could go either way, but if the light was green it meant their head teacher was happy to welcome visitors.

Every time Kristy had passed the office that morning, as she'd crossed from the humanities block to the science labs and back again, the light had been red. At last, at lunchtime, it was green. She legged it over to the door and knocked before anyone else could beat her to it.

'Come in,' said Miss Raven.

Kristy pushed the door open.

'Ah, Kristy. You must have read my mind. I wanted to speak to you.'

'You did?' Kristy pictured the hoofmarks on the playing field and the puddle on the tennis courts and braced herself for a ticking-off.

'I did indeed. Take a seat.' Miss Raven fixed her blue eyes on Kristy's. 'By letting Norah Bergman lead the team, and by riding a new horse at the last minute, you have shown both selflessness and courage, two of the attributes we pride ourselves most on here at Meadow Ridge. Our motto, after all, is Fortune Favours the Brave, is it not?'

Kristy nodded, feeling a dull flush of shame as she remembered how she'd stubbornly refused to ride Jigsaw when Emma had first suggested it.

'I wanted to let you know I'm going to nominate you for Pupil of the Year. The decision rests with the school council of course, but I like to think my recommendation carries some weight.'

'Oh, please don't,' said Kristy in a rush.

'Why ever not?' said Miss Raven.

'There must be loads of people more deserving than me. What about Ellie Brown in Year Seven? She sat in a bath of baked beans for eleven hours to raise money for the hospice! Or the sixth-formers who organised the sponsored walk? They raised loads of money for the PE department. All I did is ride, and riding is what I love to do. *Please* don't nominate me.'

Miss Raven shuffled some papers on her desk. They looked like names and addresses. Kristy dropped her gaze and surreptitiously read the top line. Centenary guest list. Her heart lurched.

'Are you absolutely sure? I have to remind you it's a great honour, Kristy. Some of our former Pupils of the Year have gone on to great things. Some of them haven't, of course. But we don't mention *them*.'

'I'm one hundred and ten per cent sure,' said Kristy emphatically.

'As a professor of mathematics, I have to tell you no such percentage exists.'

Kristy blushed again. 'Just a figure of speech.'

Miss Raven placed the guest list back on her desk. Kristy

edged forwards but she was still too far away to read it. Could she ask to take a look? Explain about Bella and Teddy and how they were her only link with Cassius? Miss Raven had seemed genuinely sorry for Kristy when she'd found out he'd been sold without her knowledge. And she thought Kristy was selfless and brave - she'd said so herself. Surely she wouldn't mind if Kristy checked where Teddy lived? Because if she found Teddy, she found Cassius.

Before she could talk herself out of it, Kristy held up her hand, as if she was still in the classroom.

'Miss Raven? You know you said you were sorry my horse had been sold and you asked if there was anything you could do to help? Well, there is.'

The headmistress looked at her inquiringly and Kristy pressed on before her courage failed her.

'His new owner...well his old owner really, but, anyway, his owner Arabella Hayward took him without me having a chance to say goodbye. Which is just the pits, because he means the absolute world to me. And now he must think I don't love him any more. Which I absolutely do.'

'So how can I help?'

'Cass is being kept at Arabella's fiancé's place, and I've no idea where it is. But I saw them yesterday at the centenary celebration. Which means one or both of them must be on your list.' Kristy eyed the sheaf of papers on Miss Raven's desk.

'You think they're past pupils?'

'They must be, otherwise they wouldn't have been invited, would they?'

'Probably not. But I have been head teacher here for nearly thirty years and I don't ever recall having taught an Arabella Hayward, I'm afraid. And I can assure you I have a photographic memory for things like that.'

Kristy didn't doubt it for a second.

'But what about Teddy?' she pressed. 'He might have been a pupil here, mightn't he?'

'Last name?' Miss Raven queried.

'That's the trouble. I don't know.'

'Hmm. We have had a couple of Edwards who preferred to be called Teddy. How old would he be?'

'Early twenties?' Kristy ventured.

'That rules out Edward Flannigan. He must be forty if he's a day. But it could be Teddy Taylor, I suppose. Can you describe him?'

'Tall, blond, drives a red sports car,' said Kristy.

'Well, he didn't have the car when he was here,' said Miss Raven with an amused smile. 'But he was tall and fair-haired. So I think he's probably your man.'

Kristy felt like whooping for joy. Instead she grinned broadly at her head teacher. 'So can I have his address?'

Miss Raven shook her head slowly and said in a grave voice, 'I'm afraid I'm not at liberty to divulge the personal details of any pupils, past or present.'

'You mean you can't -'

'Tell you his address? No. I'm sorry, Kristy, I can't.'

Kristy felt poleaxed by disappointment. To have come so far and hit another brick wall was harrowing. She slouched in the armchair, defeated.

'No,' Miss Raven continued. 'I could lose my job if I told you his address. Which reminds me, I need to pop out to the staff room for a few minutes. You'll be alright here won't you?'

Kristy nodded dully. There was nothing more to say, yet she hadn't the energy or inclination to haul herself out of the chair.

Miss Raven paused for a second by the door. 'No, it wouldn't do at all for me to *tell* you,' she said with a wink before leaving the room.

Kristy frowned. Why was Miss Raven, who was usually so severe, *winking* at her? It didn't make sense. She gazed around the room as if searching for an answer, and then her eyes fell on Miss Raven's desk. And to the pile of papers she'd left there. The list of addresses. And suddenly Kristy understood. Miss Raven couldn't give her Teddy's address - it would be unethical. But if Kristy happened to stumble upon it by chance, it was alright.

Kristy leapt out of the chair as if scalded and seized the papers. She shot a look at the door, but Miss Raven had closed it firmly behind her. She probably had a couple of minutes, tops. She licked her thumb and started flicking through, scanning every sheet for an Edward Taylor. She found him towards the bottom of the fourth sheet. She stared so hard at his address the words danced in front of her eyes. Edward Taylor, The Grange, Kingsford. It was a village about five miles out, not far from their old house.

Hearing footsteps in the corridor, Kristy quickly replaced the papers. By the time Miss Raven pushed open the door she was back in the armchair, playing with the pleats of her skirt.

'Everything alright?' the head teacher asked, a twinkle in her eye.

'Thank you for -' Kristy blurted.

Miss Raven held up her hand as if she was a lollipop lady stopping traffic. 'There's no need to say anything. It's what you do next that matters. And if you remember one thing, Kristy Moore, remember this. Fortune Favours the Brave.'

24

PRINCESS BELLA

*K*risty gazed up at the clock in the atrium outside Miss Raven's office. It was only twenty past one. If she was lucky the others might still be in the library. She hitched her bag onto her back and set off.

The glass panel of the library door was smeared with the fingerprints of a thousand students. Kristy cupped her hand over her forehead and peered inside. Sofia and the twins were at their usual table. The twins were looking daggers at each other. Sofia had her hands in the air as if she was trying to pacify them. Kristy grinned as she pushed the door open. Some things never changed.

She dumped her bag on the table and slid into the seat beside Sofia.

'Thank goodness. Perhaps you can talk some sense into them,' Sofia said, running her hands through her hair.

'I doubt it. I'm never speaking to him again,' said Norah, folding her arms across her chest.

'Why, what's happened?'

'He only went and gave me a sweet that's turned my mouth blue!'

Norah opened her mouth and waggled an undeniably blue tongue at them.

'It was supposed to be a joke,' said William.

'A joke?' Norah exploded. 'What if it doesn't come off?'

Kristy held up a hand to silence them.

'Park that. You can fight it out later. I need your help. I think I've found Cassius.'

Immediately she had their attention.

'I've managed to track down Teddy's address.'

'How?' said Sofia, impressed.

'It doesn't matter how. The important thing is I've got it. I want to go after school. But I was hoping for a bit of moral support.' Kristy paused. She wasn't very good at asking for help. Never had been. But she didn't want to go on her own. She looked at her friends. 'Will you come with me?'

'Of course we will!' cried Sofia.

'Try and stop us,' William grinned.

'How are we going to get there?' asked Norah, her hand over her mouth.

'It's in Kingsford. Not too far from my old house. We need to catch the number 47 bus. It stops in the middle of the village.' Kristy held her breath. 'Are you in?'

William clapped her on the shoulder and Sofia and Norah nodded.

'We're in!'

～

KRISTY STARED out of the bus window as the countryside sped by. Beside her Sofia played a game on her mobile phone. Behind them the twins bickered quietly. Kristy had tuned them out. She was playing different scenarios over in her head. In the first, Bella welcomed her with open arms, told her Cassius had been pining for her and pleaded with her to be a part of his life. In the next Bella was more resistant to the idea but, after Kristy poured her heart out, took pity on her and agreed. In the last Teddy sent them packing before she even had a chance to see Cassius.

A vice closed around Kristy's heart, as tight as a tourniquet. She pressed her forehead against the glass and steadied her breathing. Tears threatened, but she refused to give in to them. If she stood any chance of talking Bella around she had to be calm and matter-of-fact.

There was a hiss of air brakes and the bus pulled into a lay-by by the village green. Kristy grabbed her bag and nudged Sofia.

'This is us.'

'Ready?' Sofia asked.

Kristy grimaced. 'As I'll ever be.'

They filed off the bus and watched it rumble past the green and out of the village.

Sofia checked the time on her phone. 'The bus home stops here just after half past five. We've got an hour.'

'Where's the house?' said William.

'I don't know.' Kristy shrugged helplessly. How stupid to be so unprepared. 'Sorry.'

'Not a problem. I'll ask in there,' said Sofia, pointing a thumb at the village shop. 'They're bound to know.' She disappeared inside. Seconds later she marched back out with a grin on her face.

'It's a five minute walk up the lane beside the church. Over there. First house on the right.'

The narrow lane was flanked by hawthorns and periwinkle-blue cornflowers. Cows watched them with limpid eyes as they passed. After a couple of hundred yards the hedge to their right gave way to a flint and brick wall so tall they couldn't see over it. Kristy ran her hand along the wall and wondered if Cassius was somewhere beyond.

They reached towering wrought iron gates. A black slate sign was set into one of the gateposts. *The Grange.*

'I bet they're locked,' said Kristy.

'There's only one way to find out.' William tried the latch and the gate swung open onto a drive that swept in a generous arc towards a flint and brick house.

Kristy corrected herself. It was far too grand to be described as a house. It was a country pile, a manor house. A *mansion.*

William gave a low whistle. 'I know you said Teddy was loaded, but this is something else.'

Smart post and rail fencing skirted the gravel drive and Kristy swivelled her head from left to right as she scoured the fields beyond for a sign of Cassius. But he was nowhere to be seen.

'Looks like we're in luck,' said Sofia, pointing to the red sports car parked outside the huge front door.

Kristy took a deep breath and pulled the doorbell.

After what seemed an eternity they heard the sound of bolts being scraped back and the door was thrown open.

A slim girl in her early twenties opened the door. It was the girl from the school centenary celebration. If she was surprised to see four teenagers in school uniforms on the doorstep she didn't show it.

'What are you collecting for this time?' she drawled. 'Starving orphans or sick animals?'

Kristy took a step forward. 'Actually we're not collecting for anything, Bella.'

The girl's eyes narrowed into slits.

'What did you call me?'

'Bella,' said Kristy patiently. 'I need to talk to you.'

'Is this some sick joke?'

'Er, no,' said Kristy.

'Because if you think you're being funny,' the girl spat. 'I can tell you - you're not.'

The ground seemed to tilt under Kristy's feet as she grappled to make sense of the situation.

'You are Arabella Hayward, aren't you? Teddy's fiancé?'

'That conniving, money-grabbing little so-and-so?' The girl's eyes flashed dangerously. 'Why, are you a friend of hers?'

Kristy gaped at her. She had no idea what was going on.

Norah stepped forward and gave the girl one of her famous hard stares. 'If she was a friend of Bella's she would clearly know what she looked like,' she said smoothly. 'I'm afraid this is a simple case of mistaken identity. I assume you must be Teddy's sister?'

The girl couldn't take her eyes off Norah's blue tongue but gave a small nod.

'Then we are very sorry for the misunderstanding. Aren't we?' she said, elbowing Kristy in the ribs.

'We are. I just assumed -'

'That I was Bella? Absolutely not! I'm Beatrice, Teddy's twin sister.'

'We're twins!' William said, pointing to Norah.

As Beatrice looked from one to the other something in her face softened. 'Yes, I can see. You two would probably understand.'

'Understand what?' said Kristy, who still felt as though she'd landed in some parallel universe where nothing made sense.

'Why I was so furious to be mistaken for Bella. Right now she's public enemy number one in this house. Although I saw straight through her the moment I met her. But it's no good saying I told you so. It'll only upset him, and he's upset enough as it is.' Beatrice paused in her tirade, and looked

Kristy up and down. 'So if you're not a friend of Bella's, who are you?'

Kristy fingered the photo of Cassius she kept in the pocket of her blazer. 'It's a long story.'

Beatrice held the door open and nodded. 'I suppose you'd better come in.'

～

KRISTY FOLLOWED BEATRICE ALONG A WIDE, wood-panelled hallway into a large airy kitchen at the back of the house. The twins and Sofia were so close behind she could feel their breath on the back of her neck. Kristy quickened her pace and rehearsed what she would say. She had a nasty feeling if she didn't play it just right, Beatrice would have them out of the house before she could blink.

The older girl swept an untidy pile of magazines and books to the far end of the vast kitchen table and pulled out a chair.

'Sit,' she ordered. Kristy nodded meekly and sat at the opposite side of the table. Sofia and William sat either side of her, like trusty lieutenants at their general's side as they prepared for battle. Norah drew up a chair next to Beatrice.

The older girl lay her palms flat on the table. 'Spill the beans. Why are you here?'

Kristy reached in her pocket for the photo of Cassius. She stared at his familiar face until it blurred around the edges. Sliding the photo across the table to Beatrice she said thickly, 'Do you recognise this horse?'

Beatrice glanced down. 'Of course. It's the one Teddy bought back for Bella.'

'Not it. *He*,' said Kristy fiercely. 'Teddy had no right to buy him. He's mine.'

Beatrice frowned. 'Bella told us the horse used to be hers

but she'd given it - sorry, *him* - away. She wanted him back. I can remember the day she came over, all fired up. She'd seen him in the paper and begged Teddy to get him back for her. Teddy's totally allergic to horses - they bring him out in hives - but of course he agreed. He always did. She had him wrapped around her little finger.'

'Bella didn't give Cassius away. She abandoned him when he lost the sight in one eye. She didn't want to know. She walked away without a backward glance, leaving thousands of pounds in unpaid vet's bills and livery fees.'

Beatrice tutted. 'Princess Bella didn't want the damaged pony. Why doesn't that surprise me? So why did she change her mind?'

'Bella saw the story about us winning the quadrille. He was all shiny and new again and she wanted him back,' said Kristy flatly.

Beatrice shot Kristy a sympathetic look. 'People like Bella Hayward covet the things other people have. Teddy had a lovely girlfriend when he met Bella. But once she'd set her sights on him poor old Kim didn't stand a chance.'

'Did Teddy tell you what happened when he went to Mill Farm?' said Kristy.

'It was a bit weird actually. The first couple of times the owner denied all knowledge of the horse. But Teddy can be very persistent. And the last time he went he spoke to the owner's business partner and suddenly the horse was there after all. And this business partner was happy for Teddy to take him, as long as she was reimbursed for the money Bella owed.'

'She had no right to let him go,' said Sofia roughly. 'Cassius is Kristy's. We clubbed together to buy him for her.'

Beatrice shrugged. 'Well, she did. And of course Teddy, her knight in shining armour, bought Princess Bella her steed. It was his engagement gift to her. That and the ten grand diamond ring,' she said bitterly.

Something had been bothering Kristy and she realised what it was. 'You're talking about them in the past tense.'

'That's because Bella dumped Teddy last week. She's found a newer, richer boyfriend. Ted's devastated but he always was the soft one.'

Kristy's mouth felt as dry as unbuttered toast. She'd been so close to finding Cassius. But fate and Bella's capricious ways had conspired against her. She knew exactly what had happened. It was obvious.

'Bella's taken Cassius with her, hasn't she?'

25

TOGETHER AGAIN

*B*eatrice looked at Kristy as if she had just announced the world was flat.

'Are you mad? Of course she didn't take him with her! She took the ring and all the other presents Teddy showered her with. But the shine soon wore off the horse. He was too much like hard work. And Princess Bella doesn't like to get her hands dirty.'

'But I thought you had stables here.' Kristy waved her hands towards the huge French windows, beyond which fields shimmered like a green sea in the early evening sunshine. 'You must have grooms to look after your horses.'

Beatrice barked with laughter. 'The stables are home to a different kind of horsepower these days. My father uses them to house his collection of vintage motorbikes. There hasn't been a horse here since he was a boy.'

'So where's Cassius,' Kristy cried.

Beatrice gave Kristy a brief smile and pushed back her chair. 'Come on, I'll show you.'

~

'WHO'S BEEN LOOKING AFTER HIM,' said Kristy, worry lines crinkling her forehead.

'I have,' said Beatrice grimly. 'I told you Teddy's allergic and our parents are in the Bahamas. I don't know much about horses but it's not exactly rocket science, is it? I make sure he has fresh water, lots of grass and a couple of carrots twice a day so he can see in the dark.'

William spluttered and Beatrice raised an eyebrow.

'I was joking,' she said drily. 'I offered him a carrot one day and he seemed rather partial to it. So it became a bit of a habit.' She tucked her hair behind her ears. 'He's quite sweet actually. I've become rather fond of him.'

Beatrice seemed to spend an inordinate amount of time choosing a jacket from the many hanging on a line of hooks by the back door. Kristy hopped from foot to foot, nervous excitement zinging through her veins like electricity. At last Beatrice shrugged on a crinkly wax jacket the colour of algae and pushed open the back door.

'He's in Hastings,' she said.

'*Hastings?*' Kristy's heart plummeted. It was a town on the south east coast. Why on earth would he be in Hastings?

Beatrice chuckled. 'My great grandfather was a bit of a history buff. Named all the fields after famous battles. Waterloo, Agincourt, Trafalgar, Bosworth, you get the picture. Hastings is just the other side of the poplars.'

Kristy's patience, as taut as a tightrope, finally snapped. She physically could not wait a second longer. She broke into a run, quickening her pace until she was sprinting flat out, her legs pumping like pistons. She tore around the edge of the line of trees, flung herself over the gate and skidded to a halt, panting heavily.

There he was, grazing in the far end of the field with his back to her. Too out of breath to call out to him, she willed him to turn around, imagining her thoughts, as delicate as gossamer, spiralling through the early evening air towards him. *It's me, Cassius. I'm here. I found you.*

The big Percheron lifted his head and sniffed the wind. He whipped around, as agile as a cat despite his sturdy frame. He tilted his head and gazed at her, as still as stone.

'Cassius,' Kristy whispered.

He whinnied and Kristy's heart sang. She held out her arms and he trotted towards her, the drum of his hooves echoing the thrum of her heart. He stopped an arm's length away and she took a couple of faltering steps forward, her legs as weak as a newborn foal's. Flinging her arms around him, she buried her face in his silky soft neck and let the groundswell of tears she'd kept in check for so long finally fall.

~

KRISTY FELT a hand on her shoulder, as light as air, and a voice said softly, 'Hey, are you OK?'

Beatrice was peering at her, a worried look on her face.

'Why are you crying? There's nothing wrong with him, is there?'

Kristy broke away from Cassius, although she kept one hand entwined in his mane. 'He looks great, Beatrice. They're happy tears. I was worried I'd never see him again, you see.'

Beatrice offered her a carrot. 'I'll let you give it to him today.'

Cassius whickered and Kristy shook her head ruefully.

'I'm not sure who he's pleased to see the most, me or the carrot,' she said, half laughing, half crying.

The Percheron took the carrot from Kristy's outstretched hand and dispatched it in a couple of loud crunches. He gave a contented sigh and nuzzled Kristy's neck.

'Oh, I'd say you win over the carrot every time,' said Beatrice shrewdly.

'Cassius adores Kristy,' blurted Norah.

Beatrice smiled. 'I can see that.'

She reached into the back pocket of her jeans for her mobile and turned her back to them as she made a call.

'Teddy, you need to come to Hastings. Like right now.' She shook her head. 'No, he's fine. But there's something you need to see.' Beatrice turned back to them and rolled her eyes. 'No, it's not Bella. You know you're better off without her, don't you? We've been over this a million times. Just come, OK? For me.' She jabbed the end call icon and shoved the phone back in her pocket.

'He and I are going to fall out big time if he doesn't get that silly girl out of his system very soon,' she said archly.

Kristy could see William was struggling not to laugh.

'Do you fight much?' he asked innocently. ''Cos me and Norah never do, do we sis?'

Norah shook her head in despair. 'Of course we do. All the time.'

A flash of amusement crossed Beatrice's face. 'It's what twins do.'

Kristy ran her hands over Cassius and checked his feet. He had lost some muscle tone and needed new shoes, but otherwise he looked remarkably well. Beatrice had looked after him, there was no doubt about it. But would she be willing to let Kristy be a part of his life in the future?

She was about to broach the subject when a fit of the sneezes heralded Teddy's arrival. He trudged across the field, his blond head bowed and his shoulders hunched. Kristy felt a stab of pity for him. She knew what it was like to lose someone you loved. But then her heart hardened. He hadn't given a second thought to her feelings when he'd stolen Cassius from her. Not stolen, she corrected herself. As far as

Teddy was concerned he had bought the Percheron fair and square. It was Karen who'd betrayed her.

Teddy whipped a handkerchief from his pocket and blew his nose. He glared at his sister with puffy, reddened eyes. Whether they were the consequence of his broken heart or his allergy, Kristy couldn't be sure.

'What did you drag me over here for? You know he makes me sneeze. And who are they?' he asked, pointing at the four children, who were gazing at him in fascination.

'This is Kristy and her friends. Kristy is Cassius's rightful owner. The woman who sold him to you did so under false pretences,' said Beatrice.

Teddy shrugged. 'She can buy him back. It's no skin off my nose. He only reminds me of Bella anyway.'

A wave of hopelessness hit Kristy like a wall and she leant against Cassius. Beatrice must have noticed, as she frowned.

'What's the problem? I thought it's what you wanted?'

'I haven't got any money. I can't afford to buy him back.'

'What about your parents? I'm sure they'd stump up the cash if you asked them.'

'They would if they could but they can't. Not everyone is able to buy sports cars and ten thousand pound rings and holidays in the Bahamas. Not everyone lives in a big house like yours with fields named after famous battles and collections of vintage motorbikes,' said Kristy hotly.

Beatrice had the grace to look shamefaced. 'Point taken. I ought to know better. Our parents sent us to the local high school so we mixed with people from all backgrounds. They didn't want us growing up feeling entitled.'

With a nod of the head she motioned Teddy to join her by the band of poplars. She began talking animatedly, her hands pointing back and forth between Cassius, Kristy and Teddy. Kristy tried to lip-read but the only word she thought she recognised was 'conker' which made no sense at all.

'What do you think she's saying,' whispered Sofia.

Kristy shrugged helplessly. 'No idea.'

'It's a quarter past five. We need to go, otherwise we'll miss the bus,' said Norah.

Kristy shot a desperate look at Beatrice and Teddy, who were still deep in conversation. She held out her hand, her fingers and thumb splayed. 'Five more minutes?'

Norah sucked air through her blue teeth. 'We'll be cutting it fine.'

'My mum's at home. She'll pick us up if we miss it,' said Sofia.

'Looks like she won't need to,' William remarked. He was right. The Taylor twins had finished their powwow and were heading straight for them.

TROPHY HORSE

risty tried to read Beatrice's expression as she marched across the field but it was inscrutable. Teddy's face was hidden behind his handkerchief as he succumbed to another bout of sneezing. Kristy gripped Cassius tighter.

'I feel sick,' she said to no-one in particular.

Norah linked arms with her. 'Whatever happens, you've still got us. I know I've been a rubbish friend recently. Your heart was broken yet I was more interested in the quadrille than I was in how you were feeling. And I'm truly sorry.'

Kristy rested her head briefly on Norah's shoulder. 'That's alright. I was an idiot, too. I wanted to ride in the quadrille really but I was too proud to admit it.'

'Six to one and half a dozen to the other?' said Norah.

'That's what our mum says when we fight,' said William helpfully.

'I reckon so,' said Kristy. And suddenly her heart felt lighter. She realised she could deal with anything with her friends by her side.

Beatrice reached them, her hands on her hips. Teddy

sidled over behind her, maintaining a healthy distance between him and Cassius.

'We've talked it over and come to a decision,' Beatrice said.

Kristy held her breath.

'I think you should have Cassius back. And Teddy agrees.'

Kristy swallowed. 'But you know I can't afford to give Teddy his money back.'

'You don't need to. Cassius is yours. You've done nothing wrong, and neither did the woman at your stables. All she was doing was trying to recoup the money she was owed by Princess Bella.'

'I wish you'd stop calling her that,' said Teddy feebly.

Beatrice pulled a face. 'Whatever. And one more thing. We think you ought to have the new stuff Teddy bought Bella for Cassius. There's a new saddle and bridle, grooming kit, rugs and travel boots. He even had a mug made with Cassius's photo on it for her.'

'It's too much. I couldn't possibly,' protested Kristy.

'Oh yes you could and you will. It's our way of saying sorry,' said Beatrice. She gave Cassius a friendly pat. 'Although I might keep the mug if you don't mind? As a reminder of our time together.'

'Of course I don't!'

Teddy sneezed again. 'If that's all I'm off. Places to go, people to see. You know how it is.'

They watched him mooch back across the field. Beatrice sighed.

'I love my brother, I really do. But you know something? He's the only mug around here.'

~

KRISTY BORROWED Sofia's phone to ring Emma.

'That's fantastic news. I'm so pleased,' said her boss. The line was crackly but Kristy could still hear the smile in her voice.

'What are we going to do about getting him home?'

Kristy had been thinking about this. 'I wondered if you could ask Karen to drive over with the trailer in the morning?'

Emma chuckled. 'To hell with asking, I'll tell her. It's the least she can do.'

～

BEATRICE STARTED MAKING noises about a party she needed to get ready for so Sofia rang her mum.

'She'll be a quarter of an hour. I said we'd meet her by the village green so we'd better get going,' she told them.

'You go ahead. I'll catch you up,' said Kristy.

She wanted a couple of minutes with her horse. She smiled to herself. At one point in the dark days after Cassius had gone she never thought she would be able to say those words again. She pressed her cheek against his, closed her eyes and breathed in his heavenly horsey smell.

She broke away to gaze into his good eye. 'You're mine, all mine. And I promise I'll never, ever lose you again,' she whispered. He flicked an ear back at the sound of her voice and nodded his big, handsome head as if he'd understood every word. She wrapped her arms around his neck and sighed with happiness.

'Because it's you and me, Cassius. It always will be. You and me against the world.'

AFTERWORD

Thank you for reading *Trophy Horse*. If you enjoyed this book it would be great if you could spare a couple of minutes to write a quick review on Amazon. I'd love to hear your feedback!

ABOUT THE AUTHOR

Amanda Wills is the Amazon bestselling author of The Riverdale Pony Stories, which follow the adventures of pony-mad Poppy McKeever and her beloved Connemara Cloud.

She is also the author of Flick Henderson and the Deadly Game, a fast-paced mystery about a super-cool new heroine who has her sights set on becoming an investigative journalist.

Amanda, a UK-based former journalist who now works part-time as a police press officer, lives in Kent with her husband and fellow indie author Adrian Wills and their sons Oliver and Thomas.

Find out more at www.amandawills.co.uk or at www.facebook.com/riverdaleseries or follow amandawill-sauthor on Instagram.

www.amandawills.co.uk
amanda@amandawills.co.uk

ALSO BY AMANDA WILLS

The Lost Pony of Riverdale

Against all Hope

Into the Storm

Redhall Riders

The Secret of Witch Cottage

Missing on the Moor

The Thirteenth Horse

Juno's Foal

The Midnight Pony

The Pony of Tanglewood Farm

Flick Henderson and the Deadly Game

Printed in Great Britain
by Amazon

81691840R00103